'I won't leave you.'

'They all say that, but they all do in the end. Everybody leaves me—'

'But I won't. I won't leave you, Kate. I'll take you both with me if I have to. We'll go somewhere you're happy to be and we'll manage.'

She looked at him as if he was insane. 'You're talking as if we'd be married!' she said, and he felt the shapeless dread settle in a solid lump in his chest.

'Maybe we should be,' Sam said carefully, and to his surprise she just laughed and turned back to the window, staring out into the night.

She lifted a hand and swiped the tears away. 'You're getting ahead of yourself. You don't know me, Sam. I'm impossible to live with.'

'Baby steps, Kate. Why don't we start by getting to know each other, hmm?'

She shrugged his hand off her shoulder. 'It's not that easy—'

'Why not? How do you know? You don't know, and nor do I. But we had fun that night, Kate. It wasn't just about the sex. We talked and we laughed—and it felt real. It felt good.'

So good they'd ended up in bed for a night he still, even now, couldn't get out of his head. The night that had resulted in this baby.

Dear Reader,

When Kate first appeared on the page in *Risk of a Lifetime* I knew she was a troubled and complicated person with a lot of love to give, but damaged by her past. I had no idea what that past might be, or who the man would be who could save her from her self-destructing course.

Enter Sam, equally damaged, equally in need of healing, but for very different reasons, and also with a lot of love to give. Getting them together was easy, but how to keep them together when all either of them wanted was to run away?

Gradually, page by page, they revealed themselves to me as I unwrapped the layers of their heartbreaking pasts and found the good and decent people underneath. I just had to help them find that in each other, but it wasn't easy. I hope as you read on and learn about them for yourself you come to love them both as much as I did.

Love,

Caroline

THEIR MEANT-TO-BE BABY

BY
CAROLINE ANDERSON

First published in Great Britain 2017
By Mills & Boon, an imprint of HarperCollins*Publishers*
1 London Bridge Street, London, SE1 9GF

Large Print edition 2017

© 2017 Caroline Anderson

ISBN: 978-0-263-06713-2

Caroline Anderson is a matriarch, writer, armchair gardener, unofficial tearoom researcher and eater of lovely cakes. Not necessarily in that order. *What Caroline loves:* Her family. Her friends. Reading. Writing contemporary love stories. Hearing from readers. Walks by the sea with coffee/ice cream/cake thrown in! Torrential rain. Sunshine in spring/autumn. *What Caroline hates:* Losing her pets. Fighting with her family. Cold weather. Hot weather. Computers. Clothes shopping. *Caroline's plans:* Keep smiling and writing!

Books by Caroline Anderson

Mills & Boon Medical Romance

From Christmas to Eternity
The Secret in His Heart
Risk of a Lifetime

Mills & Boon Cherish

The Valtieri Baby
Snowed in with the Billionaire
Best Friend to Wife and Mother?

Visit the Author Profile page at millsandboon.co.uk for more titles.

Huge thanks to Sheila, my long-suffering editor, whose patience and faith in me go above and beyond the course of duty, and to my equally long-suffering husband, John, who took himself off countless times to let me wrestle with Kate and Sam, and was there for me at the end of the day with a smile and a G&T to ask how I'd got on. I couldn't have done it without you.

**Praise for
Caroline Anderson**

'When it comes to writing emotional, engrossing and irresistible contemporary romances that tug at the heartstrings, Caroline Anderson simply cannot be beaten. This outstanding storyteller has once again penned a compelling tale that is as hard to put down as it is to forget!'

—*Goodreads* on
Risk of a Lifetime

CHAPTER ONE

'SOMEONE BAIL ON YOU?'

The low voice sent a quiver through her, making every nerve-ending tingle. She knew whose it was. He'd been sitting at the other end of the bar and he'd been watching her since she walked in.

She'd noticed him straight away—hard not to, with those killer looks and a body to die for—but she wasn't looking for that kind of trouble so she'd ignored him, even though she'd been aware of him in every cell of her body. She slid her phone into the back pocket of her jeans and tilted her head back to meet his eyes.

Close to, she could see they were blue—a pale, ice blue, strangely piercing and unsettling.

There were crow's feet at the corners that might have been from laughter, or spending a lot of time outdoors squinting into the sun. Both, maybe. He had that healthy outdoor look about him, a sort of raw masculinity that sent another shiver through her body, and she lowered her eyes a little and focused instead on a mouth that was just made for kissing…

No! No way. She pulled herself together sharply. She was done with that—with all of it. She went back to the unsettling eyes.

'Is that your best shot? I've had better chat-up lines from a ten-year-old.'

Her voice sounded more brittle than she'd meant it to, but he just laughed, a soft huff of wry humour which reeled her in just a teensy bit, and those lips tilted into a smile that creased the corners of his eyes and made them suddenly less threatening.

'Sorry. I wasn't trying to hit on you. I just read the expression on your face when you answered your phone. Sort of "so what do I do now?" which is pretty much what I was trying to work out myself.'

Unlikely. Why would anyone that gorgeous have any difficulty working out what to do on a Saturday night? Not that she was interested, or cared *at all* about this total stranger, but that sinful mouth quirked again and something inside her lurched.

'I take it your other half's busy tonight, then,' she said, telling herself it was utterly irrelevant since this was going nowhere, but his mouth firmed and for a moment she didn't think he was going to answer. Then it twitched in a rueful smile that didn't quite reach his eyes.

'No other half,' he said quietly, and his voice had a tinge of sadness which made her believe him. 'The friends I've been staying with had something else on tonight, and I've got to hang on till tomorrow so I'm just killing time in a strange town, really. How about you?'

It begged an answer, and not even she was that churlish. 'I was meeting a friend,' she offered reluctantly, 'but she's been called into work.'

'Ah. My friends are having way more fun than that. They've gone to a party, so I was well and truly trumped.'

He smiled again, a wry, easy grin this time, and hitched his lean frame onto the bar stool beside her and caught the barman's eye. 'So, can I get you a drink? Since we both seem to have time on our hands?'

She did, but she didn't want to spend it with a man, and particularly not a man with trouble written all over him. She was sworn off that type for life—and probably every other type, since she was such a lousy judge of character. And gorgeous though he was, it wasn't enough to weaken her resolve. Out of the frying pan and all that. But she had to give him full marks for persistence, and at least he was single. That was an improvement.

He was still waiting for her answer, the barman poised in suspense, and she gave a tiny shrug. She could have one drink. What harm could it do? Especially if she kept her head for a change. And it wasn't as if she had anything else to do apart from tackling the mountain of laundry in her bedroom.

She let herself meet his eyes again, those curious pale eyes that locked with hers, beautiful but unnerving, holding hers against her will. They made her feel vulnerable—raw and exposed, as if they could see things about her that no one was meant to see.

Which makes having a drink with him a really bad idea.

She mentally deleted the name of the lethal cocktail she might have shared with Petra and switched to something sensible. Something safe.

'I'll have sparkling water, please.'

One eyebrow quirked, but he nodded to the barman and asked for two. So he wasn't drinking, either.

'I'm Sam, by the way,' he said, offering his hand.

'I'm Kate,' she replied, and, because he hadn't really left her any choice, she put her hand in his and felt it engulfed in something warm and nameless that brought her whole body to life. Their eyes clashed again, and after a breathless second he released his grip and she eased away and shifted on the bar stool, resisting the urge to scrub her hand against her thigh to wipe the tingle off her palm.

'So, Kate, how come you're living in Yox-burgh?'

'What makes you think I'm not passing through like you?'

His mouth twitched. 'On the way to where? It's stuck out on a limb. And anyway, the barman knows you. He greeted you like an old friend when you walked in.'

His smile was irresistible, and she felt her lips shift without permission. 'Hardly an old friend, but fair cop. I do live here. Why is that so hard to believe?'

He shrugged, his eyes still crinkled at the corners. 'Because you're young, you're—' he glanced at her ring finger pointedly '—apparently single, and it's just a sleepy little backwater on the edge of nowhere?'

It wasn't, not really, but it had a safeness about it which was why she'd chosen it, exactly because it felt like a quiet backwater and she'd thought it might keep her heart out of trouble. Except it hadn't worked.

She ignored the comment about her being single and focused on Yoxburgh. 'Actually, it's a great place, not nearly as quiet as you'd think, and anyway I love being by the sea.'

'Yeah, me, too. It's been great staying up here for the last couple of days. I'd forgotten how much I'd missed the sea.'

'So how long are you here for?' she asked, forgetting that she wasn't supposed to be showing an interest.

'Only till tomorrow morning. I spotted a boat for sale just as I was leaving this afternoon, and the guy can't see me till the morning, so I'm staying over to see if I can strike a deal.'

'What kind of a boat?' she asked, telling herself she was just being polite and wasn't really interested in the boat or anything else about him, like where he was staying or how he was going to pass the next twelve hours—

'An old sailing boat. A wooden Peter Duck ketch—' He broke off with a grin. 'I've lost you, haven't I?'

'Yup.' She had to laugh at his wry chuckle. 'Go on.'

'Nah, I won't bore you. If you don't know anything about *Swallows and Amazons* it won't mean a thing. Anyway, it needs work, but that's fine. It'll help pass the time, and I'm not afraid of hard physical work.'

She just stopped herself from scanning his body for tell-tale muscles.

'So what do you do when you're not rescuing old sailing boats?' she asked, against her better judgement. Not that she *had* a better judgement. Her entire life was a testament to that and she was still hurting from the last time she'd crashed and burned, but her tongue obviously hadn't learned that lesson yet.

He gave a lazy shrug, which distracted her attention from his kissable mouth to those broad, solid shoulders just made for resting her head against.

'Nothing exciting. I spend most of my life trapped indoors governed by unmeetable targets, and I sail whenever I get a chance, which isn't nearly often enough. Hence the boat. Your turn.'

'Me?' She let out a slightly strangled laugh and shifted on the bar stool. For some reason, she didn't want to tell him the truth. Maybe because she was sick of men running their latest symptoms by her or fantasising about her in uniform the second they knew she was a nurse, or maybe something to do with her latest mistake who'd moved on to someone brainless and overtly sexy when she'd found out he was married and dumped him? Whatever, she opened her mouth and said the first thing that came into her head.

'I'm a glamour model,' she lied, and his eyebrows twitched ever so slightly in surprise.

'Well, that's a first,' he murmured, and to his credit he didn't let his eyes drop and scan her body the way she'd wanted to scan his. 'Do you enjoy it?'

No. She'd hated it, for the massively short time she'd done it all those years ago, when she'd landed in the real world with a bump. Another mistake, but one forced on her by hunger and desperation.

'It pays the bills,' she said. Or it had, way back then.

He didn't bother to control his eyebrows this time. 'Lots of things pay the bills.'

'You disapprove?'

'It's not my place to disapprove. It's none of my business. I just can't imagine why someone with a brain would want to do it.'

'Maybe I don't have one?'

He snorted softly and picked up his glass. 'I don't think that's quite true.' He sat back, propping his elbow on the bar and slouching back against it. 'So, when you're not cavorting around in not a lot, what do you do for fun?'

She shrugged. 'Meet up with friends, read, go for walks, bake cakes and take them into work—'

'Cakes? You take cakes to the studio?'

Oh, hell, she was such a hopeless liar. 'Why not?' she flannelled airily. 'Everyone likes cake.'

'I thought models starved themselves.'

Ah. 'That's fashion models,' she said, ad-libbing like crazy. 'One reason why I could never do it. Glamour models are expected to have...'

She dwindled to a halt, kicking herself for engineering such a ridiculous conversation, and he finished the sentence for her.

'Curves?' he murmured, his voice lingering on the word and making her body flush slowly from the toes up.

'Exactly.'

His eyes did drop this time, and she felt the urge to suck in her stomach. She had no idea why. He wasn't looking at her stomach. He was way too busy studying her cleavage.

His eyes flicked away, and he drained his glass and set it down with a little clunk. 'Have you eaten? All this talk of cake has reminded me I'm starving.'

She was all set to lie again, but she was ravenous and if she didn't eat soon she was going to fall off the bar stool. Not a good look.

'No, I haven't eaten. Why?'

'Because I was debating getting something off the bar menu here, or going to a restaurant on my own, which frankly doesn't appeal. So what's it to be? Solitary scampi and chips here, or shall we go somewhere rather nicer and work on your curves? It would be a shame to let them fade away.'

No contest. She was starving and her fridge was utterly empty. 'Just dinner, no subtext,' she warned, just to be on the safe side after his comment about her curves, and he gave a strangled laugh.

'Sheesh, I don't work that fast,' he said with a grin. 'So, any suggestions for somewhere nice?'

Nice? Only one really great place sprang to mind, and judging by the cashmere jumper under the battered but undoubtedly expensive leather jacket he could afford it, but James and Connie were at Zacharelli's, and the last thing she needed was her boss asking questions on Monday morning. And anyway, they didn't stand a chance without a reservation and they were like gold dust.

His phone beeped and he pulled it out with a murmured apology and scrolled around for a moment. It gave her time to study him, to notice little things that she hadn't registered before, like the strength in his hands, the fact that he took care of them, the nails clipped and scrupulously clean. His hair was short, but not too short, and his jaw was stubbled, making her hand itch to feel the bristles rasp against her skin, right before she threaded her fingers through that dark, glossy hair and drew his head down to kiss his delectably decadent mouth…

'Sorry. I've turned it off now,' he told her, shifting his hips so he could slide the phone back into the pocket of his jeans. The movement drew her attention down, and she felt her mouth dry. 'So, any suggestions?' he asked.

Her body was screaming with suggestions, but she drowned it out. 'There's a nice Chinese restaurant on the front? In fact there are a few good eateries of one sort or another down there, so we should find somewhere with a table.'

'Well, let's go and check them out, then.' He stood up, held a hand out to her to help her off the stool and she took it, struck first by the old-fashioned courtesy of the gesture and then, as their skin met for the second time, by the lightning bolt of heat that slammed through her body at the brief contact.

She all but snatched her hand away, and then a moment later she felt a light touch over the small of her back as he ushered her through the crowd towards the door. She fastened her short jacket but his hand was just below it, the warmth spreading out to the furthest reaches of her body until there wasn't a single cell that wasn't tingling.

Oh, why hadn't she said no? This was *such* a mistake!

'Walk or drive? My car's just round the corner at the hotel if we need it.'

'Oh—walk. I know it's cold, but it's a nice evening for January, and it's not far.' And the confines of a car would be way too intimate and dangerous.

'OK. You'll have to lead the way. I'm in your hands.'

I wish...

She hauled in a breath and set off towards the seafront, and he fell in beside her, matching the length of his stride to hers as they strolled down through the town centre, their breath frosting on the cold night air.

'So what's Yoxburgh like to live in?' he asked casually, peering through the shop windows as if he could find the answer in their unlit depths.

'OK. Quiet, mostly, but there's a lot going on even so and there's an interesting vibe. I like it. It suits me.'

He turned back to eye her searchingly. 'You wouldn't rather be in London?'

No way. She'd lived in London all her life, worked there while she was training, and hated every second of it. 'No. You?'

'Oh, no, I hate it. I've been working there for a while now and I can't get away quick enough. I need a seaside town with good sailing like the one I grew up in.'

'You'd love it here, then. Lots of yachting types.'

He shot her a grin. 'I don't know that I'd call myself a "yachting" type, exactly. I just like messing about in boats. I was reared on *Swallows and Amazons*. Free spirits and all that. I guess I'm just trying to recapture my misspent youth.'

She laughed and shook her head. 'I bet you were a holy terror growing up.'

His mouth twitched. 'My parents would have an opinion on that but they didn't know the half of it. The most important lesson I learned in childhood was that you can break any rule you like, just so long as you don't get caught. What about you?'

What about her? She'd broken every rule going during her own disastrous childhood, but she wasn't going into all that with him, and certainly not on a first date. She forced herself to meet his eyes. 'I had my ups and downs.'

'Didn't we all?' he said with an easy laugh. 'I got sent to boarding school when I was ten.'

Which just underlined the differences between them, she thought. Not that it changed anything, because as soon as they'd finished dinner she'd make her excuses and leave, and that would be it.

She stopped outside the restaurant. 'Here we are, but it looks pretty busy.'

'The town's buzzing,' he said, sounding surprised.

'Saturday night, though. It's quieter midweek. There's the café next door if they don't have a table here—they do great pastries and really good coffee, so we could give it a try— Oh, hang on, those people are getting up. We could be in luck.'

He opened the restaurant door for her, and they were shown to the window table that had been vacated by the couple.

'That was good timing,' he said. 'I'm seriously starving and it smells amazing in here. So what would you recommend?' he asked, flicking the menu open.

'They do a good set meal for two, but it's quite a lot of food. We often stretch it to three. Here.'

She reached over and pointed it out, and he scanned it and nodded. 'Looks good. Let's go for that. I'm sure we can manage to do it justice. Do you fancy sharing a bottle of wine as we're not driving?'

Did she? Could she trust herself not to lose her common sense and do something rash?

'That would be lovely, but I'll only have one glass,' she said, and ignored the little voice that told her it was the thin end of the wedge.

'That was gorgeous. Thank you. I've eaten way too much.'

'Nah, you need to maintain your curves,' he said lightly, and looked down at her, at the wide grey eyes that wanted to be wary and didn't manage it, the slight tilt of her smile, her lips soft and moist and dangerously kissable.

Who was she?

Not a glamour model, of that he was damn sure, but beyond that he knew nothing. Did it matter? He hadn't been exactly forthcoming to her, either, but hey.

He leant over and kissed her cheek, brushing his lips against the soft, delicate skin, breathing in a lingering trace of scent that teased his senses and made him want more.

Much more.

'Thank you for joining me. I hate eating alone.'

'I'm used to it,' she said. 'My flatmate's moved out and it's eat alone or starve.'

They fell silent, in that awkward moment when they should have said goodbye and gone their separate ways, but he realised he didn't want to. Didn't want to say goodbye, didn't want to let her go, knowing he'd never see her again.

'Fancy a stroll along the seafront?'

There was a slight hesitation, and then she smiled. 'Why not?' she said, as if she'd answered her own question. 'I love the sound of the sea at night.'

'Me, too.'

They fell into step, and it seemed the most natural thing in the world to put his arm around her shoulders and draw her up against his side, but he could hear the click of her red stiletto boots against the prom with every step, and it was driving him crazy.

Red shoes, no pants...

The saying echoed in his head, taunting his imagination, and he tried to haul it back into order. They weren't really shoes anyway, he told himself sternly, more ankle boots, and her underwear was none of his business, but her hip nudged his with every step and it was all he could think about.

They'd walked past the cluster of restaurants and cafés and holiday flats to where the amusements started, but being out of season everything was shut and it was deserted, with nothing and no one to distract him from the click of her red stilettos.

The lights there were dim and spaced far apart, and between them there was a section of the prom that was hardly lit at all, only enough to make out her features as he drew her to a halt.

'Listen,' he said, and she tilted her head and listened with him to the soft suck of the waves on the shingle, rhythmic and soothing. In the distance someone laughed, and music blared momentarily as a car passed them and turned the corner, the silence wrapping itself around them again as the music receded.

'The sea's quiet tonight,' she said softly. 'Sometimes it's really stormy. I love it then. Wild and dangerous and free.'

'Mmm.' He stared down into her eyes, lifting a hand to stroke a stray wisp of hair away from her face. Her skin was soft, cool under his fingertips, and he let them drift down her cheek, settling under her chin and tilting it up towards him as he lowered his head slowly and touched his lips to hers.

She moaned softly and opened her mouth to him, giving him access to the touch of her tongue, the sharp, clean edge of her teeth, the sweet freshness and bitter chocolate of the after-dinner mint teasing his tastebuds as he shifted his head slightly and plundered the depth and heat of her mouth.

His body was already primed by the time he'd spent with her as they'd lingered laughing over their meal, tortured further by the nudge of her hip and the tap-tap-tap of those incredibly sexy little boots on the prom as they'd walked, and now it roared to life.

He drew away, lifting his head from hers, searching her face for clues as his heart pounded and his chest rose and fell with every ragged breath, but it was too dark to read her eyes. He could hear the hitch of her breath, though, feel the quiver in it as she exhaled and her breath drifted over his skin in tiny pulses.

'Stay with me tonight,' he said on impulse,

and she hesitated for so long he felt the sinking disappointment in his gut; but then she smiled, a wry, sad smile as she lost some internal battle and nodded.

'Your place or mine?' she murmured, and his body gave itself a high five.

They went to his hotel.

Neutral territory? Tidier than her flat, for sure, and she wasn't ready yet to give that much of herself away. Her body was one thing. Her home—that was another. So she'd told him it was further away than it really was, which made the decision easy.

The hotel was one of those anonymous places that could have been anywhere in the world, featureless but functional, scrupulously clean, the room dominated by the bed with its white striped bedding tucked tautly round the mattress.

It was hardly romantic, but it didn't matter.

All that mattered was them, alone together and driven by a need that had come out of nowhere and wouldn't be denied.

Their clothes hit the floor—jackets, her scarf, his sweater dragged off over his head so that his chest was right in front of her eyes and jammed her breath to a halt in her throat.

She reached out to touch it, her fingertips tracing the outline of taut, firm muscles that jerked at her touch. His hand caught her chin, gentle fingers tilting her face up to his, and he stared down into her eyes for a long moment before he stepped back out of reach.

'Undress for me.'

His voice was gruff, a muscle twitching in his jaw, and his eyes held hers, fire and ice dancing in their depths. Her heart was trying to climb out of her chest, jamming her breath, but she sucked air in somehow, coming out of her trance as the oxygen reached her brain and reality hit.

He thought she was a glamour model. How could she do this? Undress for him as if she had all the confidence of a woman who earned her living with her body? She couldn't even remember what underwear she'd flung on after her shower!

Matching? Probably not. The bra was hot pink, she knew that, because the lace was scratchy, and if she had that bra on, it was because she was getting to the bottom of her underwear drawer. Which didn't bode well for the knickers.

She peeled off her top, and his breath hissed in between his teeth. His hand moved as if to reach for her, and then stopped, hauled back into his pocket beside a tell-tale bulge that made her body weep and her legs turn to mush.

She sat down on the bed and unzipped her boots, tugging them off and then standing up again to slide down the zip on her jeans and wiggle them over her hips, catching a reassuring glimpse of her knickers. Navy lace shorts edged with pink ribbon, so sort of matching. It could have been a lot worse.

Easing her breath out slowly on a silent sigh of relief, she slid the jeans down, but they clung to her legs and there was no sexy way to get them off.

'Here. Let me.'

He crouched in front of her, the fabric bunched in his hands as he pushed the jeans down her legs, lifting her feet in turn to strip them away. His breath was hot, drifting over her legs, the tender skin of her thighs, seeping through the lace fabric just a hand's breadth from his mouth.

His hands slid round and cupped her bottom, holding her still as he closed the gap, breathing out, the hot rush going straight to her core.

'There goes that fantasy,' he murmured, and her ego quailed.

'What fantasy?' she asked, just so she could flagellate herself with it in the future, but he laughed softly.

'Red shoes—'

'—no pants,' she finished, and felt her breath ease out in a sigh of relief.

'I'm sure we can fix that,' he said, his voice a low rasp, but she put her hand out to stop him as he reached for them.

'Your turn,' she said, stalling for time, and he smiled wickedly and dumped his wallet and keys and phone on the bedside table before he kicked off his shoes, peeled off his socks and shucked his jeans, kicking them away to land in a heap with hers.

There was nothing unusual or remarkable about his snug jersey shorts, but the contents…

'Keep going,' she ordered, and he quirked a brow and peeled them slowly down, letting them drop to the floor as he stood there bold and un-selfconscious and gloriously naked.

How wonderful to be so sure of yourself, she thought as he pushed her down onto the bed and tipped her back, reaching out his hands to draw the dark blue lace with its pink ribbons slowly down over her hips, her legs, her feet...

'Now that's more like it,' he said, and the searing flame of his eyes stroked her with fire.

She whimpered, clenching her knees together to stop the blaze from burning her up, but he reached out a hand, pressing her knees apart, his wicked, clever fingers replacing the stroke of his eyes as his hand slid up her thigh and found its target unerringly.

The intimacy shocked and yet excited her, the tension winding tighter and tighter in her body with every touch, and then suddenly he was gone, leaving her lying there exposed and aching, screaming for release.

'Sam—?'

'Two seconds.'

She heard a slight rustle, a faint tearing sound, and then he was back. A condom, she realised. Thank God one of them was thinking straight, although he didn't need it because she was on the Pill, but she knew nothing about him—

'Shove up,' he muttered, and she wriggled into the middle of the bed as he followed her, peeling away her bra, his mouth taking its place, fastening over one breast and suckling hard as a hand found the other and cradled it in his warm palm.

His knee nudged hers apart and she yielded to him, her body aching for his, arching into him as she begged incoherently, her hesitation forgotten, pleading for something out of reach, something special, and so elusive.

'Easy,' he murmured, and then he was there, filling her, her face cradled gently in his hands as he kissed her. His mouth was hot and sweet and coaxing, his body taut and so, so clever, and the feeling inside her escalated wildly. She felt the pressure building, tried to squirm away, to stall it because suddenly to give him so much of herself seemed too great a step, making her too vulnerable to this stranger who could play her body like a violin.

He held her, though, his body claiming hers, refusing to free it, to let her escape the thing she'd yearned for and now dreaded because it would tear down her defences and leave her wide open to hurt.

'Look at me, Kate,' he demanded softly, and his eyes captured hers and held them, steady and sure, the flame burning bright as he drove her over the edge and crumbled all her defences into dust.

Then, and only then, did he close his eyes, drop his head against her shoulder and let himself go.

CHAPTER TWO

SAM PROPPED HIMSELF on one elbow and watched Kate sleeping, her rich toffee-coloured hair an unruly tangle, her limbs sprawled in exhaustion.

He knew how that felt.

Their mutual thirst was finally slaked, but on the way there he'd wrung every last gasp out of her, taken both of them to the limit of their endurance over and over again. It had been amazing, astonishing. Compelling beyond anything he'd ever felt before.

Guilt plagued him at that, but he pushed it away. It was only sex, nothing more. It wasn't disloyal, because this wasn't a relationship, just a crazy night out of nowhere. Surely to God he was allowed to have fun sometimes, to forget, just for a few hours?

A curl lay across her cheek, and he lifted it away, careful not to disturb her. Not that he thought he would. She was sleeping like the dead—

He swung his legs over the side of the bed. It was only six thirty, but the man who owned the boat was going out on the tide before nine so they'd arranged to meet at seven, but then he should be done. He could be back in town by eight, nine at the latest. Maybe she could meet him then?

Her jeans were in a heap on the floor, and her phone was lying beside them. He picked it up, and his own, went into the bathroom and called himself from her phone to get the number, then sent her a text.

Meet me for breakfast? Café by the restaurant at nine? S

He put the phones down, showered and towelled himself roughly dry, cleaned his teeth and then on the spur of the moment reloaded the new emergency toothbrush he'd found her before he pulled on his clothes and packed. He tried hard not to disturb her, but he could have slammed the door and she wouldn't have heard she was so heavily asleep. He'd ask Reception to give her a call at eight. That would give her an hour to get ready for breakfast.

He hesitated a moment, then bent, breathing in the scent of warm skin and sex as he touched his lips to her flushed, sleep-creased cheek.

She didn't move. Just as well. He was out of time.

He picked up his things, put her phone where she'd see it and let himself quietly out of the room.

A phone was ringing.

Kate struggled up out of the depths of sleep and registered her surroundings as she groped for the room phone. 'Hello?'

The recorded, electronic voice was horribly cheerful. 'This is your alarm call. The time is eight a.m.'

Alarm call? Why...?

Sam, she realised, looking round at the empty room. All his stuff was gone. He must have left for his meeting, but why hadn't he said goodbye? After all they'd shared, he'd just left without a word?

Her brain slowly coming to, she dropped the

receiver back on the cradle and slumped against the pillows.

Dammit, would she never learn?

She stumbled out of bed and opened the bottle of spring water on the hospitality tray, dragged on her clothes and shoved her phone in her pocket. She was so bone tired. She was going home for a shower and then she'd fall into bed—

Her mobile rang, and she pulled it out of her pocket and stared at it in dismay. Her ward manager, which could only mean one thing. Her finger hovered over the phone, then she gave in to the inevitable guilt and answered it reluctantly.

'Hi, Jill.'

'Kate, I'm so sorry, I hate to do this to you on your day off but is there any way you can come in?'

Again? Her heart sank and she plopped down onto the bed in despair. 'Can't you get an agency nurse? I've just done seven days straight—'

'I've tried. Please, Kate? Jane's called in—she's got norovirus, too, and we're so short-staffed we're going to have to close the Emergency Department if we can't get more nursing cover. I wouldn't ask if I wasn't desperate.'

She gave in. The winter vomiting bug had swept through Yoxburgh Park Hospital in the last few weeks, which was why Petra had been called in last night, and there was no point fighting the inevitable. 'OK, I'm on my way. I just need time to shower and grab some breakfast—'

'Quick shower. I'll make you some toast when you get here. We really need you now.'

Oh, dammit. 'OK, OK, I'm coming. Give me ten minutes.'

Which meant she didn't even have time to go home and change. It could have been worse. At least she hadn't gone out last night in a tiny dress and six-inch stilettos or she'd be doing the walk of shame.

Not that it would be the first time, she thought with a sigh, but she always kept a pair of work shoes at the hospital since the first time it had happened, and she could wear scrubs. She stripped and went back into the bathroom, and realised Sam had at least had the decency to leave her a blob of toothpaste on the new brush he'd produced for her last night out of the depths of his overnight bag. In case he ever forget to take one with him, he'd explained, proving he was way more organised than she'd ever be, but that wasn't difficult.

She cleaned her teeth with it, grateful for the burst of freshness it offered if not for his sneaky exit, then showered fast without washing her hair, wiped away the smudge of mascara under her eyes, grabbed the biscuits and water off the hospitality tray and left.

She didn't show.

He almost rang her, but stopped himself in time. She was bound to have seen the text. Maybe she just wasn't interested? Although she'd seemed pretty interested last night.

He waited until ten, dragging out his third coffee to give her time, then admitted the obvious and gave up.

It was probably just as well, he told himself, and crushed the ludicrous feeling of disappointment. He got into his car and checked his phone again. Maybe she just hadn't seen the text? But still there was nothing.

Telling himself not to be a fool, he deleted the call history and the text, threw down the phone and drove home, disappointment and regret taunting him with every mile.

It was eight that night before she finally climbed the stairs to her flat, and one glance at it made her glad they'd gone to his hotel.

Today was the day she'd set aside for cleaning it and blitzing the laundry, but that had turned out to be an epic fail. Tough. She wasn't doing it now, she was exhausted, and it would keep. She stripped, trying not to think of the way she'd undressed for Sam last night, trying not to think of all the things he'd done to her, the things she'd done to him, the way he'd made her feel.

She'd never had a night like it in her life, and it hadn't just been about the sex, although that had been amazing. It was him, Sam, warm and funny and gentle and clever. He'd made her feel special. He'd made her feel *wanted*.

Until she realised he'd just been using her.

And she couldn't really have fallen for him. Not in—what? Nine hours?

Was that all? Just nine hours? She'd wanted it to go on for ever, but it hadn't. Like all good things, it had come to an end all too soon, and he hadn't even had the decency to tell her.

She pulled her phone out of her pocket to put it on charge and saw she had a message from an unknown number.

Meet me for breakfast? Café by the restaurant at nine? S

'No-o!' She flopped back on the bed and shut her eyes, stifling a scream of frustration. How could she not have seen it?

Because she hadn't had time, was how. She literally hadn't stopped, and when she had, for twenty minutes that afternoon, she'd fallen asleep in the staffroom. She should have rung him—sent him a text, at least, to let him know she'd had to work, but she hadn't even known he'd messaged her, never mind how he'd got her number.

By ringing himself from her phone, she realised, scanning her call log.

Damn. So he hadn't just left without trace. And all day, she'd been hating him for his cowardice.

But maybe it was as well. He didn't live here,

he'd only been visiting friends, so nothing would have come of it. She didn't need to fall any further for a man she'd never see again. She would just have tortured herself that bit longer.

And anyway, she was sworn off men for life, remember? No more. Never again. Even if he hadn't just done a runner.

She hesitated, then deleted the text and the call history.

There. Sorted.

Except it didn't feel sorted. It felt wrong, leaving a hollow ache inside, but it would pass. She knew that from long and bitter experience.

Too tired to fret over it any longer, she crawled into bed and fell asleep as soon as her head hit the pillow.

An hour later she woke to a wave of nausea, a raging headache and stomach cramps, and the depressing realisation that she had the bug that had swept through the department…

It was five days before she went back to work— days in which she lost weight, grew to hate the sight of her flat and finally tackled the laundry as she waited the statutory forty-eight hours after symptoms subsided before she was allowed to return to work.

She was straight back in at the deep end, as one by one the team were hit by the virus, but after a few challenging weeks the worst of the crisis seemed to be over. It was just as well, as she hadn't really recovered her appetite and kept feeling light-headed and queasy. She staved off the light-headedness by eating endless chocolate, but she couldn't do anything about her dreams.

Too much chocolate? It had never given her any problems before, but now Sam was haunting her every night.

At first she'd been too ill to think about him, and then too busy, but it clearly wasn't as easy as all that to put him out of her mind. He was there every time she got into bed, reminding her of those few short hours she'd spent with him, making her ache with regret because she hadn't phoned him to apologise and explain.

But she hadn't, and she'd ditched his number, so regret was pointless and she was grateful when they were so busy that she was too tired even to dream about him.

And then, at the beginning of April, just over

two months after her night with Sam, she went into Resus to restock and found Annie Shackleton slumped over the desk with her head in her hands.

She and the consultant often worked closely together on trauma cases and they'd become good friends, so right from the beginning she'd been privy to the blow-by-blow development of Annie's pregnancy. Because of her husband Ed's inherited Huntington's gene she'd had IVF, so Kate had been one of the first to know the wonderful news that both embryos had taken, then that both of them were boys.

But this morning Annie had gone for a routine antenatal check, and now Kate knew something was wrong.

'Hey, what's up?' she asked softly, and Annie looked at her, her eyes red-rimmed and tight with strain.

'I've got pre-eclampsia,' she said, her voice uneven, and Kate tutted softly and crouched down beside her.

'Oh, Annie, I'm so sorry, that's such tough luck. What are they doing about it?'

'I've got to stop work. Like—now.'

'Well, of course you have, but you'll be fine! You just need to rest. Are they going to admit you?'

'Not immediately, but it's going to be so hard to take it easy. Who's going to look after the girls? I can't expect my poor mother to do any more, she's been helping me since the girls were born because I was on my own, but I only work three days a week. This'll be all day, every day, because it's the Easter holidays—and because it's the holidays Ed can't take any time off, either, because of the staff with their own children to think about. The timing just couldn't be worse—'

Her voice cracked, and Kate reached out and hugged her.

'Annie, your mum will be fine with it. She's lovely, she adores the girls and they're no trouble. They'll be falling over themselves to look after you, and Ed'll be around to get them up and put them to bed, and you know he thinks of them as his own and they love him to bits. It'll be OK, Annie. Really. You and the babies have to come first and the rest will sort itself out.'

Annie nodded slowly. 'I know that, I know

it'll be fine, but it's not just Mum and the girls I'm worried about. I'll be leaving the department in the lurch. Andy Gallagher's on holiday next week with his kids, and I have no idea how they're going to get a consultant-grade locum at such short notice—I was going to work till I was thirty-six weeks, and I'm only thirty-two.'

'So? They'll find someone. It's not your problem, Annie. It's James Slater's problem. He's the clinical lead, let him sort it out, and you look after yourself and the babies. Have you told him yet?'

She pushed herself to her feet. 'No, but I have to. You're right, the locum's not my problem—and even if it was, I don't have a choice. I'll go and tell him.'

'You do that. And go straight home, OK? I'll sort your locker out.' Kate straightened up, hugged her again and then watched her go, a lump in her throat. She loved working with Annie, and she'd miss her warmth and gentle humour. Not that the other doctors were difficult to work with, but—well, Annie had been a good friend to her, and it wouldn't feel the same without her, and she had a horrible feeling she wouldn't be coming back.

And she was being selfish. It wasn't about her.

She'd just finished restocking the drugs cupboard when James put his head round the corner. 'Annie's going home.'

'I know. She's worried about leaving you in the lurch.'

'Tough. She hasn't got a choice, and we'll cope. I'll cover it if necessary. She said something about you clearing out her locker for her. Can you put the things in my office, please, and I'll drop them off at their house on my way past tonight.'

'Will you be able to get a locum?'

He shrugged and ran a hand through his hair. 'Maybe. Connie's got a friend who seems to be kicking his heels at the moment, so he might agree. I'll get her to ring him and twist his arm. It might also mean he gets his blasted boat off our drive while he's here. Why he bought it I can't imagine, but hey. Who am I to judge? I just want it gone so we can get the house sold before the new baby comes.'

But Kate had stopped listening at the word

'boat'. Coincidence? Sam had gone to look at a boat. And his friends had gone to a party, on the same night that James and Connie had been at Zacharelli's for a fortieth. The same party?

But Sam wasn't a doctor—was he? He hadn't exactly said what he did for a living, apart from mentioning unmeetable targets—and they were the bane of most doctors' lives…

'How long's it been there?' she asked casually, her heart pounding.

'Oh, I don't know, a couple of months? It seems like for ever. Right, got to get on. Don't forget Annie's locker.'

'I'll do it now.'

Two months? That fitted. So was Sam a doctor? And if so, how would he feel about working alongside her?

Her heart gave a little kick of excitement as she headed for the staffroom and emptied Annie's possessions into a cardboard box.

Would they pick up where they'd left off?

She tapped on James's door and he beckoned her in, pointing to the phone in his hand and mouthing, 'Thank you.' She put the box on his desk as he ended the call and spun the chair towards her, grinning cheerfully.

'Job done. My sweet-talking wife just strong-armed him, and we have an amazingly well-qualified consultant trauma surgeon starting on Monday.' He tipped his head on one side and studied her thoughtfully. 'Just a word of warning, though, Kate. He's emotionally broken, so don't let his charisma reel you in. You'll just be setting yourself up for a fall.'

The word 'again' hung unspoken in the air between them, and she stifled the sigh. 'I'll bear it in mind,' she said with a forced smile, and just hoped to goodness it wasn't Sam because if it was, the warning might have come too late to save her.

She was off the next day, and she popped round to Ed and Annie's house on the cliff to see how Annie was doing.

'She's fine, before you ask,' Ed told her with a smile as he let her in. 'I'm pampering her to death. She hates it.'

'I bet she doesn't really. I brought her flowers to cheer her up.'

'Thank you. She'll love them. She's out in the garden with the girls because it's such a gorgeous day. Go on out. I was just making us coffee. How do you like it?'

'Can I have tea?' she said. 'White, no sugar?'

'Sure. We've got cake as well. I'll bring it out.'

She found Annie on a lushly padded swing seat under a canopy, her feet up and the girls chasing each other round the garden. Annie waved at her, and she went over and gave her a hug and handed her the flowers.

'Oh, how gorgeous, you sweetheart! They're so pretty. Thank you. I'll get Ed to put them in water. It'll give him something to do apart from clucking round me like a mother hen.'

She pulled her legs up out of the way to make room, and Kate sat down and settled Annie's swollen feet onto her lap.

'So, how are you? You look the picture of contentment.'

Annie smiled. 'I feel it. It's wonderful—and even better now I know James has found a locum who can actually do the job properly. Ed's driving me slightly nuts, but the girls have been as good as gold, and if the babies would both stop kicking me to bits I could really relax! Feel them—it's like a football team warming up. I can tell they're boys.'

Kate laughed and laid her hand over Annie's bump. 'Good grief. They're having a rare old shuffle, aren't they?'

'It gets a bit crowded in there with twins. It was the same with the girls, but I think these two are bigger. Is Ed bringing you a coffee?'

'Yes—well, tea. I can't drink coffee since I had the bug.'

'That's months ago! You're not pregnant, are you?' she teased.

She laughed. 'Don't be ridiculous. How could I be pregnant? I've sworn off men—and anyway, I'm on the Pill and it's only coffee I don't like. I think I've just had too much of it.'

Annie laughed and rolled her eyes. 'That hasn't put you off chocolate!'

'Or cake,' she said with a chuckle. 'No, it's just the bug.'

But when Ed brought the tray out then and put it down right next to her, the smell of coffee drifting towards her on the warm spring air made her gag.

Could Annie possibly be right? How likely *was* it that she'd still be feeling ill two months later? Not at all…

But she couldn't be pregnant. There was no way. It could only have been Sam, and anyway, she'd done a pregnancy test. Unless…

'Cake?' Ed asked, cutting into her thoughts. 'My grandmother made it. It's her trademark lemon drizzle and I know you'd prefer chocolate but I've never known you turn down cake of any denomination.'

'Thanks. It sounds lovely,' she said, not really paying him attention because her mind was tumbling.

Because she was on the Pill they'd thought it was OK when his condoms ran out, and it would have been, without the bug, but it had dragged on for days, too long for the morning-after pill to work, so she'd done a test and it had been negative. She hadn't given it another thought at the time, but now…

The girls went back to their playhouse and Ed took the tray inside, but she hardly noticed until Annie shook her shoulder.

'Kate? Are you OK? You look as if you've just seen a ghost.'

Or realised that her worst nightmare might actually have come true...

Annie's eyes widened as she stared at her, and she could see the moment her friend's thoughts caught up with her own. 'Oh, no. You're not, are you?'

She started to shake her head in denial, and then shrugged. 'I don't know. I don't think so. I'd put it down to the bug, but it's possible...'

'Oh, Kate. Do you want to do a pregnancy test? I've got a spare one upstairs in our en suite.'

'I've already done one, ages ago, and it was negative—and anyway, I can't just go up there to your bedroom!'

'It's fine, I'll take you up. I need to put the flowers in water and if Ed asks I'm showing you the nursery.'

So they went, dumping the flowers in a vase on the way, and she took the test Annie handed her, closed the bathroom door and bit her lip. Did she want to do this? Yes! Heavens, yes, she wanted to; she needed to know, and as fast as possible, just to put herself out of her misery.

And there it was, in black and white. Well, blue, really, she thought inconsequentially, staring at the wand as she dried her hands on autopilot.

Pregnant. It didn't tell her how pregnant, and her mind tried to sort it out. It was the beginning of April, and she'd met Sam at the end of January. So…nearly nine weeks ago, which made her eleven weeks pregnant, maybe? Her other test must have been too soon…

'Kate? Kate, are you OK?'

She opened the door, her hands shaking as she held out the wand to Annie. 'You were right,' she said, her voice sounding hollow and far away. 'Oh, God, Annie, what on earth am I going to do?'

She felt arms come round her, the firm jut of Annie's pregnant abdomen pressing against her. She could feel the babies kicking, and with a shock she realised that if she did nothing, then in a few more weeks this would be her, her body swollen by the child growing inside it.

And then what? How could she be a mother? She had no idea what a mother even *was*. Not a real mother.

Her teeth started to chatter, and Annie tutted and sat her down on the bed, putting her arm around her and rocking her. She could remember her foster mother doing that when she was sixteen, trying to soothe her when her world had been turned upside down and all feeling had drained away.

It felt the same now, the same numbness, the same emptiness and *what now?*-ness that she'd felt then.

'I can't do it, Annie. I can't do it on my own—'

'Do you know who the father is?'

She nodded. 'Yes, of course I know. Hell, Annie, I'm not that reckless, but I can't contact him. I don't have his number any more, but he won't want to know, it was just one night. Oh, God, I've been so stupid! Why…?'

'Hush, hush,' Annie crooned, rocking her gently. 'It'll be all right. You can do it. I did it on my own.'

'No, you didn't, you had your mum, and I don't have a mum—'

'But you have me. I'll help you. You won't be alone, Kate. And you can do this, if you decide you want to. You'll be all right.'

And if she didn't want to?

If Sam really *was* the locum, she'd have to tell him, and then he'd have an opinion, want a say. He might want her to go through with the pregnancy even if she decided that she couldn't. And if the locum wasn't Sam, she'd deleted all trace of him from her phone, so she wouldn't be able to tell him, however much she might decide she wanted to.

Which meant if she kept it she *would* be all on her own to deal with it, bar a little help from Annie.

But that was fine. She'd been on her own most of her life, and she liked it like that. She'd had enough of being bullied and manipulated and lied to.

Not that Sam would necessarily do any of those things, but she wasn't inclined to give him the chance.

Even assuming Sam *was* the locum.

He was.

She knew that the moment she walked into the department two days later, at seven on Monday morning. She heard his laugh over the background noise, heard James saying something and then another laugh, and it drew closer as she turned the corner.

She ground to a halt, too late to turn and walk away, too shocked to keep on moving past because she hadn't really believed it would be him. And then he saw her and his eyes widened in surprise.

She searched his face, fell in love with it all over again and then remembered all the reasons she had to regret that she'd ever met him. One in particular...

'Ah, Kate. Let me introduce you to Sam Ryder, our locum consultant. Sam, this is Kate Ashton, one of our best senior nurses.'

'Hello, Kate,' Sam said softly, but speech had deserted her and the ground refused to swallow her up. 'Do you two know each other?' James asked after an uncomfortable silence.

'Yes—'

'No!'

They spoke in unison, and James did a mild double-take and looked from her to Sam and back again. 'Well, which is it?'

Sam just stood there, and after a second she

found her voice. 'We've met,' she qualified. 'Just once.'

Just long enough to make a baby…

A muscled clenched in his jaw, but otherwise Sam's face didn't move. No smile, no frown—nothing. Just those accusing eyes.

She felt sick. Nothing unusual. She was getting so used to it, it was the new normal.

The silence hung in the air between them, broken only by the sound of a pager bleeping. James pulled it out of his pocket and scanned the message.

'Sorry, I need to go. Sam, why don't I put you in Kate's hands for now and let her show you round? She's worked a lot with Annie so she's the expert on her role, really. I'll see you later. Come and find me when you're done with HR.'

James clapped him on the shoulder and walked off, and Sam's eyes tracked him down the corridor and then switched back to Kate. She'd forgotten how piercing they could be.

'You didn't tell me you were a nurse.'

'You didn't tell me you were a doctor.'

'At least I didn't lie.'

She felt colour tease her cheeks. 'Only by omission. That's no better.'

'There are degrees. And I didn't deny that I know you.'

'I didn't think our...'

'Fling? Liaison? One-night stand? Random—'

'Our private life was any of his business. And anyway, you don't know me. Only in the biblical sense.'

Something flickered in those flat, ice-blue eyes, something wild and untamed and a little scary. And then he looked away.

'Apparently so.'

She sucked in a breath and straightened her shoulders. At some point she'd have to tell him she was pregnant, but not here, not now, not like this, and if they were going to have this baby, at some point they *would* need to get to know each other. But, again, not now. Now she had a job to do, and she was going to have to put her feelings on the back burner and resist the urge to run away.

She pulled herself together with effort and straightened her shoulders. 'So, shall we get on with your guided tour? What have you seen?'

'His office. Nothing else, really.'

'Right. Let's start at Reception and work through the route the patients take, and then you can go up to HR. I'll give you a map of the hospital.'

And with any luck her legs wouldn't give way and dump her on the floor before they were done...

'We need to talk.'

There was a lull in the chaos that had been the day so far, and they were alone at the desk, filling in paperwork on the last case. He paused, his pen hovering over the notes.

'We do?'

He was still stinging a little from her rejection back in January, not to mention her denial to James that she knew him, and he'd spent the whole morning so far trying to quell his traitorous body, which seemed to be delighted at her sudden reappearance in his life. In fact she'd been at least half of the reason he'd taken this locum job, on the off-chance that he might run into her again, but now he had it seemed like a profoundly lousy idea, especially since they were going to be working together.

He made himself look at her, forced himself to meet her eyes instead of avoiding them as he had been.

'I wouldn't have thought we had anything to say.'

She flinched a little, but held her ground.

'There's a lot to say.'

'Like why you didn't answer my text?'

He saw her throat bob as she swallowed. 'I didn't get it—not until much later.'

'That's a lie. I saw it on your phone when I sent it so I know it arrived.'

'But *I* didn't see it on my phone. I didn't have time to check until I got home—I was called in to work that morning.'

'Sure you were.'

'Why do you have to think the worst of me? I'm not lying, and it's on record.' She bit her lip, but her eyes looked troubled, and she gave a frustrated little sigh. 'Look, Sam, I don't want to do this here. Can we meet up later? Please?'

He propped himself against the desk, hands rammed in the pockets of his scrubs so he didn't reach out to her, and studied her, trying and failing to read her expression. 'OK,' he conceded finally, massively against his better judgement—although where Kate was concerned he didn't seem to *have* any judgement. 'What time do you finish?'

'Three. You?'

'Technically five, but maybe later. We could go to a pub, I suppose,' he offered grudgingly, but she shook her head.

'No, not a pub. Where are you staying?'

'With James and Connie, but there's no way you're going there.'

She frowned. 'No, definitely not.'

'Where, then?'

She bit her lip again and he felt almost sorry for it. 'My flat?' she offered, sounding as reluctant as him. 'You could come round when you finish. Six o'clock-ish?'

He nodded, relieved that they were going somewhere private. 'OK. Give me the address. Oh, and you'd better give me your phone number again in case I'm held up.'

She nodded, and he couldn't help noticing that she looked wary. Almost—hunted?

'Kate, I get that it was a one-night stand,' he muttered, relenting a little. 'I'm cool with that, and I didn't want any more. I don't,' he added, feeling a twinge of guilt at the lie. 'But you could have answered my text.'

'And said what? Thanks for a great night, sorry I missed the chance to say goodbye when you *sneaked out of the hotel room*?'

'I hardly sneaked—'

'You could have woken me up. You could have just asked me—' She broke off and gave another impatient little sigh and pulled the phone out of her pocket. 'Tell me your number.'

She keyed it in, and his phone vibrated in his pocket. 'OK, I've got it,' he said, and put it into his contacts. 'I'll call you when I finish, give you a head's up.'

'I'll text you my address. It's the top-floor flat. Number three.'

She hesitated a moment, then turned away, leaving him puzzled and a tiny bit intrigued.

She probably wanted to set the ground rules for their relationship, he decided.

Well, that was easy. Hands off. He could do that.

He went back to work.

CHAPTER THREE

SHE STOOD AT the bedroom window and watched a car pull up outside the house right on the dot of six, and she ran downstairs and opened the front door.

'You found me OK, then?' she said, stating the obvious, but he just gave her a quizzical smile.

'It's hardly rocket science. I've got a satnav.'

Of course he had. Her stomach in knots, she turned away without another word and led him up the narrow, winding staircase that rose to the top floor of the big Victorian townhouse. Once upon a time it had been elegant. Now it had a run-down feel to it, as if it had been a long time since anyone had truly loved it, and she wondered what Sam with his privileged upbringing would think of it. Not that it mattered.

She'd left the door at the top standing open, and he followed her in, past the cramped kitchen into the sitting room that seemed suddenly much smaller with him in it. It was shabby without the chic, but thanks to the last two hours of frantic activity it was at least clean and tidy, apart from the shelves in the alcoves, which were overflowing with books.

'Drink?' she asked, stalling for time, and he nodded.

'Yeah, thanks—I could murder a coffee.'

No chance. She waved at the sofa. 'Make yourself at home. The kettle's hot, I won't be a moment.'

She closed the kitchen door, sucked in a deep breath and tried to steady herself, to slow the heart that was lodged in her throat.

'You can do this,' she whispered, but she didn't know how, didn't know if she would ever be ready to say the words that would change their lives for ever.

He looked around, trying to get a handle on her character, but there was nothing to give her away.

No ornaments or photos, the tired furniture showing evidence of a long, hard life, but at least it was clean.

He studied the books, but all they proved was that she had eclectic taste.

Biographies, travel guides, romance, crime, historical sagas, a collection of cookery books—and a small children's book, dog-eared and tatty but presumably much loved.

What did she want to talk about?

He heard her come back in and turned, searching her face and finding no clues. She set the tray down and handed him a mug.

He glanced at it, then sniffed it experimentally. 'Is this tea?'

'Sorry, I ran out of coffee. Anyway, you've been drinking it all day and tea's better for you.'

That made him blink. 'Are you trying to mother me?' he asked, mildly astonished because she hadn't seemed like the sort of woman who'd hold back on anything if she wanted it, far less advise anyone else to, but he must have hit a sore spot because she sucked in her breath and looked away.

'Don't be ridiculous. Why would I do that?'

'Search me. Kate, what did you want to talk about?'

She met his eyes, looked away briefly and seemed to brace herself before she spoke again.

'OK. I do have coffee, but I can't cope with the smell of it at the moment.' Her eyes locked with his, defiant and yet fearful, and her next words took the wind right out of his sails.

'I'm pregnant.'

There. She'd said it.

And from the look on his face, it was the last thing Sam had been expecting to hear.

He turned away, put the mug down on the mantelpiece and gripped the shelf so hard his knuckles turned white.

'How?'

His voice was harsh, brittle, as if he was holding himself together by sheer willpower. She could understand that. She'd been doing it ever since she'd found out, and she felt as if she hadn't breathed properly for days.

'We ran out of condoms, remember? That last time.' The time she'd assured him it was safe. The irony of it wasn't lost on her.

She saw him frown in the mirror. 'But you told

me it was OK. You said you were on the Pill—
or is that another lie?'

'No! I am on it—or I was. But I went down
with norovirus right after work and I couldn't
even keep water down for days.'

'You're sure? You're not just…'

'I'm quite sure. And trust me, I'm no more
thrilled about it than you are.'

'You know nothing about me or my feelings,'
he growled, lifting his head and meeting her
eyes in the mirror. 'Nothing.'

'I know you don't mind breaking rules so long
as you don't get caught.'

He held her eyes for a moment, then looked
away. 'Not that one. I never, ever break that one.
I'm fanatical about contraception.'

'Apparently not fanatical enough.'

She sighed and reached out a hand to him,
then dropped it in defeat. 'Sam, we can't fight.
This isn't going to go away just because we don't
like it.'

He rammed a hand through his hair and turned
to face her. 'Are you *absolutely sure* it's mine?'

She felt her skin blanch. 'Of course I'm sure—'

'Really? Because you fell into bed with me

readily enough and you were already apparently on the Pill.'

'Which makes me just as much of a slut as you. If I remember rightly, you had condoms in your wallet just in case.'

He winced, and she nodded. 'There. Not nice, is it? But it's the truth. Neither of us knew anything about the other, and everything we thought we knew was lies. But we've made a baby, Sam,' she said, her voice starting to crack. 'I'm eleven weeks pregnant and we have to make a decision—'

His head jerked back as if she'd slapped him, and she saw him swallow. 'You want to get rid of it?'

She blanched, the words were so blunt, but her feelings were so confused, so chaotic she couldn't analyse them. 'No— I don't know. All I really want is for this never to have happened, and believe me, if I could wind the clock back it never would, but it has, and...'

'So why didn't you contact me? Why leave it to now to make a decision? It doesn't make sense.'

'I didn't know! I only found out two days ago.'

'I don't believe that. You must have noticed your cycle—'

'I don't have a cycle. I take it continuously, and I did a pregnancy test after the bug, which was negative—and anyway, I didn't have your details. I'd deleted them from my phone and I had no way of contacting you. I didn't know who you were. All I knew was your first name.'

'Are you sure? Because you didn't look surprised to see me this morning, which makes me think you knew who I was all along.'

'I didn't! I didn't have an inkling until a few days ago when James said something about you working as our locum might mean you got the boat off their drive, and I started to wonder then, but he didn't mention your name and I didn't know for sure until I saw you. How was I supposed to know? You hadn't told me you were a doctor. You hardly told me anything...'

She tailed off, finally running out of words, of breath, of any hope of an easy resolution, and just like that her emotions imploded. She felt her eyes prickle, felt the sob lodge in her chest as the fear and loneliness and desolation of her childhood rose up to swamp her.

'I can't do this, Sam,' she said, pressing her eyelids together to stem the tears but instead squeezing them out so that they trickled down her cheeks, laying her soul bare. 'I can't do it. I don't know how. I just want it all to go away…'

How could he not have seen this coming?

It was so obvious now, but it hadn't even been on his radar when she'd said they needed to talk. Perhaps it should have been.

God, he'd been such a fool! He wished he'd had the sense to walk away, right after they'd come out of the restaurant—or sooner, before he'd started the conversation that had ended up with them making a baby, of all things—

She'd turned her back on him but she was too late. He'd seen the fear in her eyes, the tears she'd tried so hard not to shed, and he wanted to comfort her, but how, when he himself was screaming inside? What could he say that would make it better? Nothing.

Nothing at all, because nothing short of a miscarriage or termination was going to make this go away, and even then they'd both carry the scars for the rest of their lives.

'Kate—'

He couldn't go on, didn't know what to say, but he couldn't just stand there watching her shoulders shake as the sobs she couldn't hold back racked her body. His feet moved without his permission, his hands coming up to turn her into his arms, cradling her against his chest.

He felt her crumple, felt the fight go out of her as she sagged against him, and he stood there and held her and wondered what kind of a god had done this to him, to them.

To give him his dream, everything he'd always wanted, everything he and Kerry had planned, but with a woman he didn't know, didn't love, while the woman he loved lay cold in her grave—

'Come and sit down,' he said gruffly, leading her to the sofa and half sitting, half falling into it with her still in his arms while the pain exploded in his head.

He hadn't realised he could still hurt, that anything else could possibly have touched that deep, dark place inside him left by Kerry's death, but this had ripped it right open and he felt as if he was drowning in pain.

* * *

She didn't know how long they'd sat there. All she'd been aware of was the tension in him, the rigidly controlled breathing, the reflexive stroke of his thumb against her shoulder.

What was he thinking? He hadn't said anything, and she had no idea what was going on in his head. As she'd rather cruelly pointed out that morning—was that all? It seemed a lifetime ago—they only knew each other in the biblical sense. Not nearly well enough to read his mind.

She shifted, easing away from him, and his arm dropped from her shoulder as she disentangled herself and stood up, pacing to the window and staring out, arms wrapped tight around her waist, holding herself together.

At some point during the evening it had started to rain, and she watched the water dribbling down the rippled Victorian glass and wondered how to break the agonising silence that stretched between them.

'So what now?' he asked, his voice a little rough, gritty with emotion as he broke the silence for her.

Now? 'I have no idea,' she said woodenly. 'I'm

still coming to terms with it. I haven't really had time to think.'

'Does anyone else know?'

'Only Annie Shackleton.'

'The woman I'm covering for?'

She nodded. 'She sort of guessed. It was the coffee thing. I usually drink gallons of it and I can't bear it now. She said it as a joke, but it turned out not to be so funny.'

Understatement of the century.

She heard him move, saw his reflection in the window as he crossed the room and stood beside and behind her. His hands were rammed in his back pockets, his posture defensive. 'So what do you want to do? You said you can't do it— was that just fear talking, or do you really mean it?'

She couldn't see his eyes, and she realised she needed to, so she turned and looked up at him and then wished she hadn't, because she could see the faint sheen of unshed tears, and there was a muscle jumping in his jaw, as if he was hanging by a thread.

She reached up a hand and touched his face,

and he flinched and turned his head away. Her hand fell back to her side and she bit her lip.

'What do you want me to do?' she asked, her voice sounding hollow to her ears.

He gave a soft huff of something that wasn't quite laughter and turned back to her, his eyes dry now and oddly devoid of emotion.

'You really want to know? I want you to evaporate, never to have existed. I want that I hadn't gone into that pub, that you hadn't come in, that I hadn't talked to you, taken you for dinner, taken you back to my hotel and spent the night getting *biblical* with you. But I can't have what I want. I can only have what is, and what is is that you're pregnant with my child, and like it or not—and I'm guessing neither of us do—we're going to have a baby. So I will do what I have to do. I'll stand by you, and I'll be a part of my child's life for ever, because I don't have a choice.

'I can't walk away, I can't live the rest of my life pretending this hasn't happened, and although I can't stop you having a termination if that's what you really want, I'll do everything in my power to try and convince you not to. I'll even bring it up on my own, if that's what it takes, but I will do the right thing, by you and by my child.'

Kate stared at him in astonishment. 'You'd do that? Bring the baby up on your own?'

'Of course—and so would you, if you had any decency.'

She felt panic fill her at the thought, an overwhelming dread that swamped her. She reached behind and gripped the window frame, propping herself against it for support.

'Sam, I—I couldn't. I have no idea how to look after a child. How to mother one. I don't even know what a mother *is*!' she said, her voice rising in panic. 'What if I failed? What if I did something dreadful and damaged the child for life? What if one day I realised I just couldn't do it and walked away and left her there—what then? What would happen to that child?'

'I would be there,' he said firmly. 'Always. Every day. And you wouldn't fail—'

'How do you *know* that? You can't know that. And when I do, the damage—do you know what it's like when your mother walks away? Leaves you, five years old, in the care of total strangers? Just—leaves you?'

* * *

She's talking about herself. Dear God—

'Kate...'

He reached for her, drew her shaking body into his arms, cradled her against his chest. The tight band around it loosened, easing as he held her, the contact somehow freeing him from the grip of helplessness that had taken hold of him when she'd told him he was going to be a father.

Because he wasn't helpless now. He didn't want this, but he could do it, and he *would* do it, because that was who he was. OK, he'd broken rules, but never the important ones until now, and at the end of the day he'd always known his duty and carried it out without question. And he knew his duty now.

'We'll be OK,' he told her. 'Somehow, we'll find a way. I'll look after you—'

'I don't need looking after!' she protested, pushing away from him. 'It's not me I'm worried about! It's the baby! I can't let anything bad happen to it—'

'And nor can I. So we'll look after it together—'

'How? You're only here for a few months, a

year at the most, and then you'll be gone. You'll leave me—'

'I won't leave you.'

'They all say that, but they all do, in the end. Everybody leaves me—'

'But I won't. I won't leave you, Kate. I'll take you both with me, if I have to, if I can't find a job locally. We'll go somewhere you're happy to be, and we'll manage.'

She looked at him as if he was insane. 'You're talking as if we'd be married!' she said, and he felt the shapeless dread settle in a solid lump in his chest.

'Maybe we should be,' he said carefully, and to his surprise she just laughed and turned back to the window, staring out into the night.

'You're crazy,' she said, but her voice had a little shake in it and he could see the tears trickling down her cheeks.

'Maybe. Or maybe I'm just being honest. We need to be together to do this, and maybe that's the best way.'

She lifted a hand and swiped the tears away. 'You're getting ahead of yourself. You don't know me, Sam. I'm impossible to live with.'

He gave a short, mirthless chuckle. 'I've been in the army for years, Kate. Believe me, I can live with anyone.'

Anyone except Kerry, the only person I want to live with...

He slammed the door on his grief and reached out a hand, laying it gently on her shoulder. 'Baby steps, Kate. Why don't we start by getting to know each other, hmm?'

She shrugged his hand off her shoulder. 'It's not that easy—'

'Why not? How do you know? You don't know, and nor do I. But we had fun that night, Kate. It wasn't just about the sex. We talked, and we laughed—and it felt real. It felt good.'

So good they'd ended up in bed for a night he still, even now, couldn't get out of his head. The night that had resulted in this baby.

He put his hand back on her shoulder. 'We have to try. At the very least, we have to try.'

He felt the muscles in her shoulder bunch, then relax as the fight went out of her. 'OK,' she said. 'One week. I'll give it one week, and if I don't think I can do it…'

'Then we'll talk again,' he promised, vowing

that there was no way they'd get to that point. If pregnancy hadn't been on his radar earlier, it was now, and there was no way on God's earth he was going to let her do anything to harm their child. He'd just have to make it work.

But—one week? How the hell could he turn this around in a week? His stomach growled, dragging him back to the here and now, and he rammed his hands into his pockets.

'Have you eaten?'

'Eaten?' She shook her head. 'No. I'm not hungry.'

'You have to eat—'

'The baby's fine!' she snapped, spinning round and glaring at him, and he arched a brow.

'I'm not worried about the baby, I'm thinking about you. You've been working all day, the flat smells of furniture polish and bleach so I know you've been cleaning it ever since you came home, and I haven't eaten either. So—takeaway, or go and find somewhere to eat?'

She looked at the window. 'We'll get soaked.'

'No, we won't. The car's right outside and we'll go somewhere with parking.'

'Isn't Connie going to be expecting you for supper?'

'No. I told them I'd make my own arrangements.'

For an age she stood there, staring out at the rain streaming down the windowpane, and then she nodded.

'OK. But I'm paying for myself.'

He opened his mouth to argue, shut it again and held her coat for her. She took it, resisting even that gesture, and shrugged into it. 'Come on, then, if we must.'

He took her to the Chinese restaurant on the front, partly because he knew she liked it and partly because he knew it wasn't expensive and he had a feeling he'd lose if he tried to argue with her about the bill.

'This is where we started,' she said bleakly as they were shown to the same table, and he found a smile for her. It wasn't much of one, but it was a start, and frankly it felt like a miracle that he could smile at all.

'So it is,' he murmured, and took her hand, running his thumb over the back of it in a soothing sweep. 'It'll be OK, Kate,' he told her softly. 'We'll make it OK.'

He just wished he could see how.

By mutual agreement, they didn't tell anyone.

Annie knew, of course, but she didn't know who the father was, and Kate didn't tell her. It didn't seem appropriate, really, to share any more than she already had about a baby whose fate hung in the balance.

The days ticked by, but they didn't work together, not after that first day. James, she imagined, was keeping them apart because Sam was, as he'd put it, 'emotionally broken'.

How? Why?

She found herself more and more curious about that, about what had broken him so badly that the news of her pregnancy had almost reduced him to tears. Because he wasn't a crying man, she was sure of that. He'd been in the army for years, he'd said. Men in the army didn't shed tears lightly.

So—what had happened? Or who?

But it never seemed like a good time to ask something so sensitive, and so they carried on, passing in the corridors, their shifts barely co-inciding, and in the evenings he came to her flat and they talked about anything but the baby and her childhood and whatever it was that had broken him, and the days ticked by.

They took it in turns to cook and she learned that he was a good cook, way more house-trained than she was, that he ate whatever was put in front of him and thanked her for cooking it—even though sometimes it was a bit hit and miss.

And he didn't touch her.

Didn't brush against her, didn't kiss her cheek or pat her shoulder or give her a hug or squeeze her hand—nothing. And sometimes, just when she thought he might be going to reach out for her, his eyes went blank and he looked away.

Until she tripped on the stairs.

It was Friday night, and for once they'd finished their shifts at the same time. He'd given her a lift home, picking up a takeaway on the way home, and as she was running up the stairs ahead of him she caught her toe on the worn carpet and fell.

'Ouch—dammit!' She sat down on the stairs,

cradling her wrist, flexing it warily, and he hunkered down beside her.

'You OK?'

'Yes, I'm fine,' she said, flexing it again, but it made her gasp and she felt his warm, firm hands take her arm and feel carefully, thoroughly down the bones in her forearm to her wrist.

'Does that hurt?' he asked, but she was so mesmerised by the warmth of his touch that she could hardly feel anything else.

'No. It's OK now—just a bit hyperextended, I think. It'll be fine.'

'You need ice on it—'

'No ice.'

He picked up her bag and the post she'd dropped and scattered all over the stairs, shooed her up the last half-flight and raided the little freezer compartment in her fridge. 'Peas—they'll do. Got a sandwich bag?'

She gave up any hope of independence and pointed. 'In the drawer.'

Five minutes later she was sitting on the sofa with her arm resting on a cushion, a small bag of peas wrapped in a tea towel perched on her wrist, a loaded plate in her lap and a steaming mug of tea by her side.

'If you've put sugar in that I'll kill you,' she said mildly, and he chuckled.

'I don't think you're suffering from shock.'

She sighed. 'No. Just terminal clumsiness and stupidity.'

'Actually the carpet's worn on that tread.'

'Sam, it's been worn since I moved in three years ago. It's hardly a novelty.'

He grunted, plonked himself down beside her, adjusted the peas on her wrist and picked up his own tea. Not coffee. In deference to her nausea, he didn't drink it if she was around, which, did he but know it, earned him a shedload of brownie points.

'Can you manage to eat that?'

'What are you going to do, feed me? Of course I can manage.'

'Just asking,' he said, sounding mock-aggrieved, and she chuckled and picked up her fork with the uninjured hand.

'Don't worry, Sam. I won't starve. It's not in my nature.'

He grunted and dug into his food, then took

the plates out and came back and sat down, her letters in his hand.

'Want me to open your post for you?'

She felt herself stiffen. 'Why would you do that?' she asked, suddenly wary, and as if he realised he rolled his eyes.

'To save your wrist? I wasn't going to read it— just open it and give it to you, but that's fine, go ahead and struggle one-handed,' he said, and dumped it on her lap, but it slid to the floor at her feet.

She stared down at it lying there, feeling silly now for making a fuss. 'Sorry. I just have issues with boundaries.'

'A controlling ex?' he asked, and she laughed bitterly.

'No. Just a boy who didn't respect my privacy and went out of his way to make my life difficult.' A boy who'd hated and resented her and ruined the only decent chance at a family life she'd ever had...

He nodded, then picked the post up again and handed it to her. 'Don't worry, your boundaries are safe with me. I just didn't want you to hurt yourself.'

She handed it back—as an olive branch? Maybe. 'I'm sorry. Would you?'

And then she instantly regretted it, because the first one out of the envelopes was her ultrasound appointment, and it was so obviously an appointment letter that he couldn't help but notice.

'My twelve-week scan,' she said, because to say nothing wasn't an option. 'I saw the midwife on Tuesday. She said it would be soon.'

There was a second of silence before he spoke. 'Can I come?'

Her hesitation was longer than his, her fear almost suffocating her because she knew once she'd had the scan it would all become so real that there would be no hiding from it. 'I don't know...'

'That's fine. Just let me know when you've worked it out. I'd like to, if I may, but I fully appreciate it's your decision.'

Did he? She had a feeling the words were choking him, but there was nothing she could do about that. She wasn't at all convinced she wanted him there. She didn't want to be there, either, but she had no choice. He, on the other hand...

'Is this just so you know how old it is, so you can rule yourself out as the father?' she asked, suddenly uncertain of his motives, but his hissed expletive set her straight.

'I thought you'd know me better than that by now?' he growled.

'No, I don't,' she said sadly, 'and you don't know me, either, but you're talking about us living together and bringing up a baby, and all the while we're dancing round each other at arm's length and avoiding any kind of contact and it just feels so cold and remote and unemotional and I just can't read you when you're keeping such a distance. I don't know who the hell you are, Sam, so how can I know if I can trust you?'

'I was just giving you space,' he said quietly, after her words had hung in the air for an age.

'Me, or you?'

'Both, maybe,' he admitted, and she searched his eyes.

'Maybe I don't want space.'

His breath hissed out in a sharp sigh.

'Kate, don't say that. It's hard enough keeping my distance as it is. That's why I've been holding you at arm's length, because I don't trust myself around you, at least not until we know where we stand. We really don't need to add the confusion of a physical relationship to this equation, it's complicated enough.'

She sighed. 'I know, and I do understand that, but it just seems so—lonely,' she said plaintively, despising her weakness but sick to death of the endless distance between them.

But then he gave a quiet sigh and buckled. 'Come here,' he said softly, and taking the letter out of her hand, he wrapped an arm around her shoulders and eased her up against his side.

She could feel the solid warmth of his body, smell the scent of his skin and a trace of the aftershave that had haunted her all week, bringing back so many memories of the night they'd met, and she wanted to burrow into him and stay there.

'This doesn't change anything,' he murmured, the sound rumbling through his chest.

'That's a shame,' she said, before she could stop herself, and she felt rather than heard the soft chuckle.

'Yeah, it is, but it's not a good idea, Kate, not

with so much at stake. We need to take our time with this.'

'I thought you'd want to hustle me into bed and sweet-talk me into keeping the baby,' she said, almost disappointed, and this time the laugh was a sad huff of despair.

'You really don't think a lot of me, do you, if you think I'd sink so low that I'd use sex to manipulate your feelings?'

'Most men would.'

'I'm not most men. I'm just me, trying to do what's right for all three of us, and frankly I don't know what that is. I feel as if I'm groping my way along a narrow ledge in the dark, and it's scaring the hell out of me.'

He sounded so lost, so lonely that she lifted her hand and cupped his cheek, feeling the rasp of his stubble against her palm and longing for him to kiss her, to bring back the closeness she'd felt on that January night.

'I swear I didn't do this on purpose.'

He turned his head slightly and kissed her hand, sending shivers of need through her. 'I know you didn't. It's not your fault. It's mine. I'm the one that broke my golden rule, not you.'

'It's not all your fault—'

'Yes, it is. It's all down to me, and it's my responsibility to fix it and I don't know how right now.'

'I really did think it was safe,' she told him, hating that he was taking the blame when all the time it was just a wicked twist of fate. 'And I know this is hurting you.'

His body stiffened fractionally and although he didn't move she felt the gulf open between them again. 'Why would you think that?'

'Your reaction? I'd expected you to be angry when I told you, but you were more upset.'

'I was just shocked.'

'No, you weren't. It was more than that, much more, as if I'd hit a raw nerve. And before you started James told me to steer clear of you because you were emotionally broken.'

This time he went rigid, his body unyielding, frozen. 'Why would he say that?'

'I have no idea. That's all he said, but I have a gift for choosing the wrong men. Maybe he was just trying to protect us both, but he didn't say what from.'

He disentangled himself, getting to his feet

and walking to the window, his back straight, hands rammed in his pockets as he stared out into the night, and she watched his reflection in the glass and held her breath for what felt like an age.

'He's right, I suppose,' he said eventually, his voice expressionless. 'My fiancée died two years ago, just before our wedding.'

For the first few seconds shock held her rigid, then she stumbled to her feet and crossed over to him, wrapping her arms around him and holding him tight.

'Oh, Sam, I'm so, so sorry...'

She crushed down the tears, the sobs. This wasn't her grief, it was his, and she needed to be here for him. But he didn't want her. His body was held rigid, but she didn't let go. She couldn't let go, couldn't abandon him now when it was all so raw because of her forcing him into a corner and making him drag it all back up out of the past.

'I'm sorry,' she said again, her voice a whisper in the silence, and then at last he moved, as the tension eased out of him on a ragged sigh, turning to haul her hard against his chest.

They didn't speak, just stood there holding each other as their emotions came under control again. And then he let her go, easing away a fraction, cradling her face in his hands as he stared down and searched her eyes, his own empty and desolate.

'Don't pity me, Kate,' he warned softly. 'I don't want your pity. It's not about you. It's about me, and it's nothing to do with us, with this—situation we're in.'

She nodded, willing her tears not to overflow now, but it was hard, and she took his hands and lifted them away from her face and went into the kitchen. 'I'll make some more tea,' she said, her voice a little thickened, and she filled the kettle and started to wash up, but her wrist gave a twinge and she gasped.

'Let me do that.'

'It's fine, I can manage.'

'I'm sure you can, but you don't need to. You don't have to prove anything to me—'

'I'm not proving anything to anybody. I'm just washing up. It's hardly going to kill me—'

Her words echoed in the sudden silence, reverberating around them like a tolling bell, and then he swore and headed for the door.

She heard it slam and the sound of his footsteps running down the stairs, and still she didn't breathe. *What had she done? Why had she said that, of all things?*

The last thing she'd meant to do was hurt him with her careless words. It must be horrendous for him being stuck with her when all he wanted was—she didn't even know her name, the woman he'd lost and was still obviously grieving.

'Oh, Sam,' she said softly, and it was only after she heard the outer door close and saw his car drive away that her eyes welled with tears.

Not for herself, but for the lonely, broken man she was in danger of falling in love with, and the nameless woman he'd loved and so cruelly lost.

The wind had strengthened, and it would have made sense to have picked up his coat on the way out, but he didn't care about the cold, or the sting of the sea spray that bit into his cheeks as he strode along the darkened prom. He walked from one end to the other and back again, hands rammed in his pockets as the wind tugged at him, the sound of the sea crashing against the shore drowning out his furious tirade as he vented his anger and grief and frustration.

It was just all so *wrong*, so horribly, horribly wrong, and despite his duty, despite knowing what he had to do, it was only now that he realised the implications of what he'd said to her on Monday when she'd first told him she was pregnant.

He'd virtually promised to marry her, but how could he do it, how could he make those same vows he'd been going to make to Kerry? He couldn't stand there by the altar and wait for the wrong woman to walk down the aisle to him, her body cradling his child.

It should have been Kerry! Kerry, whom he loved with all his heart. Kerry, who should have been walking down the aisle to him...

They'd buried her in the wedding dress she'd never had the chance to wear, and he'd lifted the veil from her face and put the wedding ring on her lifeless finger before he'd kissed her goodbye, so pale, so beautiful. So dead.

He screwed his eyes up to shut out the images,

but they wouldn't leave him, and now alongside them was the image of Kate's face, racked with dread and apprehension as she'd told him she was carrying his baby.

There was no place for her there with the images of Kerry, but there she was, intruding on his grief without even trying, trashing everything when he'd just got his life back on an even keel.

Or thought he had, but now he realised he'd been kidding himself; he wasn't over Kerry, hadn't dealt with her death, he'd just been running away, and he was in no way ready to take on the responsibility for another woman and a child.

Which made no difference at all, because he and Kate had both messed up, and now there was an innocent baby to consider who hadn't asked for any of this and didn't care if they were ready or not.

There was nowhere else to run to. It was time to face reality, to put the past behind him and move on.

CHAPTER FOUR

SHE WAS ALONE in the locker room the next morning when he walked in and she turned to him, racked with guilt.

'Sam, I'm sorry—'

'About last night—'

They spoke together, and he ran a hand through his hair and let out a short huff of something that could possibly have been laughter. Or despair.

'I'm sorry,' she said, before he could speak again, because the look on his face had haunted her all night. 'Sorry I said that, sorry I pushed you to tell me about her, just—I'm sorry. So sorry. I had no idea—I would never have—'

'Forget it. You didn't make it any worse, Kate, it is what it is. And I'm sorry I left like that. I shouldn't have walked out, I just needed some air.'

She nodded her understanding and then, just because she had to do something other than stand there, she opened her locker and turned back, his coat in her hand.

'You left this behind.'

'I know. I got more fresh air than I bargained for,' he said wryly, taking the coat. 'Thanks. How's your wrist?'

'Oh.' She glanced at it. She hadn't even given it a thought she'd been so distressed. 'It's fine. I'd forgotten.'

'The power of frozen peas,' he said, his mouth tilting into the beginnings of a smile as he lobbed his sweater into the locker and turned the key, and she hauled in a shaky breath.

'Well, I'd better get on,' she said.

'Yeah, me too. I'll see you later. How about a coffee, if we can find time?'

He wanted to spend time with her? She felt her shoulders drop in relief, and she smiled at him. 'Yes, that would be good. Where are you working?'

'I think I'm in Resus.'

'Oh. So am I. James must have run out of ways of keeping us apart.'

A fleeting frown crossed his face. 'Do you seriously think he's been doing that?'

'Well, one of you has. It certainly wasn't me.'

'Nor me.' His mouth flickered in a smile. 'Ah, well, I'm sure he'll get over it. Shall we go and face the fray?'

He held the door for her, and she walked past him, close enough to smell the mint on his breath and see the tiny cut where he'd nicked his skin shaving. She wanted to reach up and kiss it better, but thought better of it and made herself keep moving.

It was busy all morning, without time to draw breath never mind take a break, and then just when they were thinking about grabbing a coffee it all kicked off again.

'Adult resus call, cardiac arrest, ETA five minutes,' a disembodied voice announced over the PA, and she went to the desk to find out more.

'Twenty-year-old male, no known history. He was playing football,' she was told. She turned towards Resus and nearly bumped into Sam.

He was standing right behind her, his face a mask, and she took his arm and moved him away from the desk.

'Are you OK?' she asked softly.

'Why wouldn't I be?'

The eyes were still blank, as if he was in lock-down, and she gave a tiny, questioning shrug. 'I don't know, you tell me.'

His eyes snapped to life. 'I'm fine. Let's just do it, please?'

There was no time to discuss it further, because the doors from the ambulance bay flew open and their patient was wheeled in, a paramedic kneeling over him doing chest compressions.

Sam was straight into it, taking over CPR from the paramedics as they wheeled the patient into Resus, listening to their report, firing the odd question, issuing instructions in a calm, clear voice as he delegated tasks to the hastily reassembled team.

James was in there too, working on another critical patient, and he lifted his head and frowned.

'Want to swap?' he asked Sam, but Sam shook his head.

'I'm fine.'

'OK. If you change your mind—'

'I won't.'

So it wasn't just her imagination. There was something wrong—something to do with his fiancée's death? Whatever, James was there in the background, so she stopped fretting and concentrated on doing her job for their patient. Frankly, he needed everyone's concentration, and even so she didn't think they'd save him, but Sam refused to stop, and so she and the rest of the team shrugged and kept going, too.

They'd been working on him for thirty minutes without success when James came over, his own patient now stabilised.

'Do you think you should call it, Sam?' he murmured, but Sam shook his head.

'No. Not giving up.'

Just that, but there was a world of pain and resolution in his terse reply, and James just nodded and took over chest compressions, letting Sam call the shots as he stayed there, ready to take over if he did crack, but he didn't.

It seemed for ever before the young man's heart finally restarted, by which time he'd been down for fifty-five minutes and they had a senior cardiologist and a team from CCU standing by to take over. Only then did Sam step back, his face drained.

James laid a hand on his shoulder.

'Good call, Sam, well done. Kate, you two go for coffee now, I'll hand over and talk to the parents,' James said softly, and she wheeled Sam out into the fresh air, waiting as he stood for a long moment, hands rammed in his pockets, hauling in air.

'OK now?' she asked when he let the air out on a long ragged sigh, and he nodded.

'Yes, I am now we've got him back. I just wasn't going to let him go without a fight.'

'No, I realised that. Come on, let's get you some coffee.'

He nodded again and walked with her round the outside of the building to the café.

'Stay here, I'll get it,' she said, and went in and ordered a coffee for him and a bottle of water for herself, added a double chocolate muffin and carried it out to him, her mind tumbling with questions she couldn't ask.

He was leaning against the side of the building, one foot propped up on the wall, arms folded, and he shrugged away from the wall and crossed over to her, taking the coffee from her. 'Sorry, I shouldn't have let you go in there. I know it makes you feel queasy.'

'Actually it was fine. It's getting better. Want to sit outside? It's peaceful but the benches might be a bit damp.'

'I'm sure we'll cope. Is that muffin for me or are you going to make me watch you eat it?'

'I had thought we'd share it,' she said, turning her head and looking up at him, and he smiled slowly, his eyes crinkling slightly at the corners, the tension receding.

'Thank you.'

'It's only half a muffin.'

'I didn't mean the muffin.'

'Oh.' *Then what...?* 'Here, this bench looks OK.' She sat down, patted the space beside her and he perched on the edge and propped his elbows on his knees, the coffee dangling from his fingertips as he stared vacantly at the floor. Seeing what?

'Want to talk about it?' she asked, when he'd sat there for several seconds without moving.

'Not really. Nothing to say.'

'You saved his life, Sam. That's not nothing.'

'I wasn't talking about Tom. And he's not out of the woods yet by a long way.'

'No, I don't suppose he is, but at least he has a chance now, thanks to you.'

They fell silent, and she watched him as he fought some inner battle and finally gave in.

'We were due to get married three weeks after I came home on leave from Afghanistan,' he said, his voice sounding rusty and unused. 'Kerry emailed me, full of all the things we had to do before the wedding, bubbling with excitement, telling me she couldn't wait to see me, but there was an army officer waiting for me when I landed.'

Kate felt her heart thud, her breath jamming in her throat as he went on.

'Her family had raised the alarm the night before because they couldn't get hold of her, and she was found dead in our flat the morning I landed. No warning, no symptoms, nothing. The post-mortem revealed an undiagnosed heart condition that had led to a cardiac arrest. And just like that, it was all gone. My whole life—all our plans for our wedding, the family we were going to start—everything, wiped out when her heart stopped beating.'

And if you'd been there, you might have saved her...

Sam took a long pull on his coffee, wiped his mouth on the back of his hand and leant back with a sigh. 'If only I'd been there, Kate,' he said softly, as if she'd spoken out loud. 'If only I'd come home a day earlier, or it had happened a day later, I might have saved her. I could have kept her going, like I kept Tom going, until her heart had restarted, but I never got the chance.'

She felt her eyes well with tears. 'Oh, Sam. No wonder you couldn't let him go,' she said softly. 'Would you ever have given up on him?'

He shrugged. 'I don't know. Maybe, when I couldn't go on any longer? When the team had deserted me, and James had dragged me off his body? I don't know. Luckily we didn't have to find out. So, are we eating that muffin or are you just going to pull it to pieces?'

She looked down at it, the paper case shredded, a big chunk of the cake broken away in her fingers. She took the chunk, handed the rest to him and swiped the crumbs away impatiently.

'Here, you eat it. I've had far too much cake recently as it is. My clothes are all getting tight.'

'Is that just from cake, or could it be the baby?'

'Maybe. I would have thought it was too soon, but—possibly.'

'When's your scan?'

'Monday. It's at eight in the morning.'

'Do you want me there?'

She turned and searched his face, wondering how he could bear to do this, how he could even look at her after what he'd told her about Kerry's death. 'Do you still want to come?'

'I do, but I thought you didn't want me there.'

'I wasn't sure last night. It seemed odd, as if you were a total stranger, but now, since you've told me about Kerry, let me in a bit, I feel as if I know more about you, about where you're coming from on this. Enough at least to know that even though you obviously wanted a family, having a baby with me isn't something that you would have signed up to in a million years, and that you deserve a say in what happens to it.'

'Is that still in the balance?'

She looked away, her heart pounding suddenly. 'I don't know. So—will you come? I'm not sure I want you in with me, but—maybe, just in case...?'

Something a little desolate flickered in his eyes, and then he nodded. 'I'll be there. I said I would, and I don't break my promises.'

He pulled his watch out of his pocket, glanced at it and swore. 'Come on, we need to get back. I've got a shedload of paperwork to do for Tom.'

He drained his coffee, crumpled up the muffin case and lobbed it and the cup into the bin.

'Do you need to debrief?'

Sam sighed quietly and swung the chair round so he could see James. 'Why does everyone think I need to talk about it?'

James dropped into a chair and tilted his head on one side. 'Everyone?'

'Well—Kate, anyway.'

'Ah. Yes. Kate. How well do you know her?'

Well enough to make a baby.

'Hardly at all. I met her the night I stayed over to see the boat guy. I'd checked into a hotel, went for a drink, she was in the pub. We had a meal together.'

James gave him the unnervingly level stare

that was his trademark, and Sam held it with effort.

'She's a nice girl,' his friend said quietly. 'She's got a ridiculously kind heart and appalling judgement, which is a lousy combo. She doesn't always make good decisions.'

No. She hadn't done that weekend, anyway, or they wouldn't be in this—no. Not mess. Situation. To call it a mess wasn't fair to the baby, and didn't really sum up the full implications. He wasn't sure 'situation' did, either, but he wasn't getting into any of that with James.

'She is a nice girl. She said you'd been keeping us apart. And that you'd told her I was broken. Cheers for that.'

James winced. 'Ah, yes. That. I was just—'

'Warning her off?'

'She's—vulnerable. And she's been hurt badly in the past. A married man, the archetypal love rat, amongst others.'

He winced. 'Did she know he was married?'

'No. She had no idea, and she was devastated. Like I said, she's a lousy judge of character where men are concerned, and she had a troubled childhood, too. Life's been pretty crap for her, really. She's had a lot to deal with.'

'So I gathered, but haven't we all?' he said, making a mental note to delve more into her past. 'You, me, Connie. We've all lost someone we loved.'

'I guess so, but that was different. We haven't been betrayed, and, anyway, you're still grieving so a complicated person like Kate is the last thing you need.' James stood up and laid a hand on his shoulder. 'You know, you don't have to eat out every night. You're more than welcome to join us. Connie was complaining she wasn't seeing enough of you.'

He gave a soft laugh. 'Early days yet. She'll soon be sick of the sight of me. I'll be around tomorrow. I'm off all day, I thought I'd work on the boat.'

'OK. Just…'

'Just?'

'Be careful with Kate. I know you're seeing her, you can't keep anything private in a hospital no matter how discreet you are, but I don't want to see either of you get hurt.'

Too late. In just six months, God willing, he

and Kate would have a baby. Too late to worry about not getting hurt. The repercussions were off the Richter scale.

'Don't worry, James,' he lied, wondering why the words didn't choke him. 'We're taking it nice and slowly.' Now the damage was done…

James grunted, patted his shoulder again and went out, and Sam went back to work.

'James warned me not to hurt you today.'

Kate blinked and turned towards him, vegetable knife in hand. 'Really?'

'Yeah. I told him what you'd said about me being broken, and—well, basically he justified it by telling me that you have crap judgement where men are concerned and you had a crap childhood and don't mess with you.'

She sighed crossly and went back to hacking up the carrots. 'He really is the soul of discretion. I don't know where he gets his nerve.'

Sam laughed and hugged her, then took the knife off her and shouldered her gently out of the way. 'He's all right. He means well. I think he's very fond of you. What are you making, by the way?'

'A stir fry—and I doubt that he's fond of me, more likely worried I'll cause trouble.' She sat down at the table and let him take over the veg prep, since he was doing such a good job of it. 'So what else did he say about me?'

The knife kept moving. 'Something about a married man—no details, just that he was the archetypal love rat.'

'Hmph. Nicely summed up. He was a locum radiologist, and he—well, let's just say he never mentioned his wife, and when I found out, he moved on to an agency nurse with bigger boobs. The only comforting thing was that at least mine are real.'

That made him laugh, as it was meant to, but he shook his head as well and gave her a wry glance over her shoulder. 'I don't know how you can joke about it. I would have happily killed him for you. And, for what it's worth, there's nothing—*nothing*—wrong with your body. Any of it.'

He looked away before she could read his expression, but his words had left her with a warm glow, and she nursed a secret smile for a moment.

'So how well does James know you?' she asked, and he shrugged and carried on slicing.

'A bit. Connie knows me better, but they were both there for me when it got really tough and I owe them.'

'How did you meet them?'

'At her first husband's funeral. He was a bomb disposal officer, and when Saffy got caught up in a controlled explosion, Joe felt really guilty, and he brought the dog to me. He shouldn't have done it, Saffy should have been shot at the scene, but we cleaned her up, Joe nursed her back to health and everyone kept shtum while he tried to get her brought home.

'And then he got caught in another blast. I was the first medic on the scene, and I watched him bleed out into the sand with not a damn thing I could do about it. His body was flown home with some injured men, and I went to his funeral. Connie was there, obviously, and so was James. He'd known them both for years, introduced them to each other, apparently. Anyway, then she came out to Camp Bastion and worked alongside me to try and make sense of the senseless waste of life. I'm not sure she managed it, or if any of us ever do, but we became friends, and Kerry and I went to their wedding, and when Kerry died they were there for me. Like I said, I owe them.'

'Gosh. No wonder they care so much about you. I haven't got any friends like that. Well, maybe Annie.'

'Shackleton?'

She nodded. 'She's been great since I found out about the baby. Really supportive, but I was there for her when she and Ed were going through a tough time. Do you know he's got the Huntington's gene?'

He frowned over his shoulder. 'Really? But she's pregnant.'

'I know, but he's only a carrier, he won't get it, and they had to have IVF to screen the embryos, which was pretty gruelling. I'm so happy for them. Ed wanted kids so much—well, that's pretty obvious since he's a paediatrician. I guess you and Kerry wanted them, too, from what you've said.'

He stopped slicing, turned towards her and leant back against the worktop, his hands rested on the edge. 'Yeah. Yeah, we did. Me, probably, more than Kerry. It was the driver behind us getting married rather than just carrying on as we were, but as it turns out, she probably wouldn't have survived pregnancy anyway with her heart condition.'

'Oh, Sam.'

She got up and went over to him, putting her arms round him and leaning into him, her head on his chest. 'I'm sorry.'

'Yeah, me, too. It's ironic that I've sort of got my way in a way I would never have imagined.' His arms came round her, and he rested his head on hers. 'I'm sorry I got you into this situation, Kate. I know it's the last thing you want, but I really mean it, I will be here for you, and one thing you can be sure of, I'm not a love rat.'

She nodded, and lifted her head to meet his eyes. They were gentle, full of regret but also sincerity, and she knew she could believe in him. She just wished she could believe in herself.

'I know that.' She kissed his cheek, stepped back and picked up the knife. 'Come on, I'm starving, let's get this food cooked.'

* * *

The next day was glorious, so he went out early for a run along the sea wall with only the gulls for company.

He didn't have to worry about Kate, because she was working the morning shift and wanted a quiet afternoon alone—to think about what the next day might bring? Very likely. He would have done. Which meant he had no excuse not to spend the day tackling the boat as he'd said.

Not that that task wasn't long overdue. Time to have a really, really close look at what he'd bought, and while he was doing that he could try and get his head round how he felt about Kate.

Confused, mostly, although his body wasn't. He was still aching to drag her into his arms at every opportunity, and only an iron determination had stopped him from talking his way into her bed last night, but he needed distance from her until she'd made her decision. If she decided on a termination—

Dammit, he couldn't let her do that. Although he had no idea how to stop her. No right to stop her. That was the really scary thing. And yet, having seen her with patients, he knew she was soft-hearted and filled with the sort of kindness and warmth that made a perfect mother. Maybe she just didn't realise it?

He put it out of his mind and got the tools out that James had more than cheerfully lent him that morning. He was standing on a ladder stripping paint off the wooden hull and trying to assess the condition of the timber when Connie came out. She stood at the bottom of the ladder peering up at him, shielding her eyes from the sun.

'Coffee time,' she said firmly, and he turned off the blowtorch, put the scraper down and joined her on the ground in the litter of paint curls.

'It really is a heap,' she said, eyeing the boat doubtfully. 'Are you sure you can turn it around? Or were you trying to set fire to it? I take it it *is* insured?'

He sighed and dragged a grubby hand through his hair. 'I'm sorry. It was a sort of spur-of-the-moment thing and if I'd know you'd want to move I wouldn't have landed it on you.'

'To be fair to you, we didn't know at that point. You could always just sell it,' she added after a slight pause, and he tried to ignore the hopeful note in her voice. But her bump was growing by the day, and they really did want to move before their second child arrived. And much as he loved it, he had to admit the boat was an eyesore. Not to mention clogging up the drive.

'I'll get rid of it, Connie, I promise, one way or another. They might have room for it in the boatyard now it's spring. Where's Saffy?' he asked, changing the subject.

'James took her out for a walk with Joseph. Come on, I'll make you a nice strong full-fat coffee and you can keep me company while I drink my decaf one. The joys of pregnancy,' she said with a laugh over her shoulder as she led him up the steps to the veranda on the back of the cottage, and he felt a surge of guilt for keeping Kate's pregnancy secret. Not that it was his secret to tell.

'James said you had a bummer of a sticky case yesterday,' she said as she handed him his coffee.

He shrugged and blew on the coffee, taking his time. 'It had a good outcome. He's alive, at least, and under the care of the cardiology team, so he's got a fighting chance now.'

'Are you OK?'

'Yes, I'm fine. Really. Don't worry about me, Connie. I'm a big boy now.'

'I know that. Doesn't stop me worrying. It must have been a bit close to home.'

He wouldn't have taken that from anyone else, but, as he'd told Kate, they'd seen each other through hell.

'Sam?'

He gave a quiet sigh. 'You don't need to protect me, Connie. I'm fine.'

'Are you? You've been looking kind of preoccupied. And—I know you have the right to have fun, to play the field a bit to balance the books, and I'd hate you to grieve for ever, but—don't mess about with Kate, Sam, please?'

He might have known she had an agenda. No sooner did she have him captive, settled on the veranda with his feet up on the rail and a steaming mug of coffee in his hand, than she'd started. He shook his head slowly.

'Why not? We're both adults, she's alone, I'm alone, it's someone to pass the time with—'

'You could pass the time with us. We hardly ever see you.'

'Are you jealous?' he asked, knowing full well she wasn't, and she punched his shoulder lightly.

'Don't be an idiot.' She shifted so she could look him in the eye better. 'Don't hurt her, Sam—'

'Why does everyone feel the need to protect her from me?' he asked, exasperated and racked with guilt.

'Because she ricochets from one disaster to another and she'll fall for you, I know she will. You're just her type—funny, sexy—but you're broken, Sam, you know you are, and she'll end up hurt, all over again. She's a brilliant nurse, but her private life's a nightmare and I can't bear to see her hurt.'

Too late, Connie...

'I'm sure we're both grown up enough to sort out our own salvation,' he said drily, hoping it was true and that tomorrow didn't go disastrously wrong after her scan.

He heard the gate clatter, and knew he had just about five seconds to move before James came and joined in the nagging fest. 'Right, back to the boat,' he said hastily, but he was too slow. His feet hit the floor just as Saffy came racing up the veranda steps and launched herself at him.

'Get *down*, you horrible dog, you have no manners,' he said mildly, fending her off and rubbing her head affectionately as he stood up to make his escape.

'I see you found the tools,' James said, appearing at the bottom of the steps with Joseph on his shoulders, and Sam sighed inwardly.

'Yeah. Don't worry, Connie's already had a go at me. I'm on it.'

James quirked an eyebrow, but Sam ignored it. He was well aware of the pressure he was under. It didn't need reinforcing, and he had other more important things to worry about.

'Can you do me a favour, while I think about it?' he asked James. 'I need an hour off in the morning for an appointment. Is that OK?'

'Yes, sure—unless you want to swap shifts? I'm doing two to ten today, but Connie's arranged to view a house this afternoon which I really want to see, and she's busy tomorrow, so it would suit me fine to swap.'

'Sure.' It suited him far better, because he'd be

able to give his attention to Kate. 'It does mean I won't do any more to the boat this afternoon.'

'I'm sure one more day won't make a difference, Sam. And there's always tomorrow.'

He nodded, knowing full well that Kate was off all day and after the scan they'd have a lot to talk about. She'd given him a week, and it was up tomorrow evening. He had one last day to convince her she could trust him, and there was no way the boat or anything else was getting in the way of that.

CHAPTER FIVE

NOTHING FITTED.

She'd spent the last week working in scrubs, but now she needed something to wear for her scan, and that meant trousers and a top, and none of her jeans went within a mile of doing up.

Well, an inch, at least, but that was bad enough. Too much cake and chocolate, she told herself, because the other reason was still a little unreal and she wasn't ready to face it.

She found some stretchy denim jeggings and a loose top with a long cardi over it, which hid her little bump nicely, to her relief. She didn't want anyone at the hospital to guess. Not yet, not until she knew for sure that she'd go through with it.

She put a scarf on for good measure, wrapping it loosely round her neck so it hung down the front and helped with the disguise. It also covered up the little bulges where she was bursting out of her bra, and she realised she was going to have to go shopping very soon—maybe later today.

Unless…

Her hands flew down to cover the little bump that she could no longer ignore, her fingers curling protectively over it as panic swamped her.

Today was D-day. The day she'd told Sam she'd give him her decision. She'd said that she'd give him a week, and what did she know about him now that she hadn't then? What did she know that made a difference to her ability to cope with this?

More, sure, but enough to base a life together on? *Enough to trust him with her heart?*

Maybe she didn't need to. Maybe she could just trust him to care for the baby with her, to make sure that she didn't go wrong, didn't fail, didn't run away like her mother had.

And if she couldn't? When it came to the crunch, what if she couldn't do it, couldn't bond, couldn't cope? Sam had said he'd have the baby, but what if he realised that he couldn't handle it, and left? Left her, like everyone else, but this time literally holding the baby?

Would it be kinder to her baby not to be

brought into a world with so much uncertainty and instability? A world like the one she'd been thrust into at the age of five?

She sucked in a breath, met her eyes in the mirror and looked away, unable even to look at herself any more she was so torn with guilt and self-loathing.

Time to go. She couldn't be late, and it was a ten minute walk if she hurried. Damn. She shrugged on her coat, picked up her keys and ran downstairs, opening the front door just as Sam lifted his hand to ring the bell.

'You're here,' she said unnecessarily.

'Yes. I've been here ten minutes. I thought you were leaving it a bit late, so I just wanted to check you were OK.'

'I'm fine,' she said, her eyes unable to hold his. 'I'm going to walk.'

'You haven't got time, Kate. That's why I'm here, so you don't have to.'

'We can't go in together! What if we're seen?'

'What of it? What difference does it make?'

None. Everyone must know by now that they were seeing each other, but not in the antenatal department—

'Can we go in through different entrances? Just to...you know.'

He shrugged and opened the car door. 'Sure. Come on. I'll drop you off and meet you in there after I've parked the car.'

She nodded, and he held the door for her—that bone-deep politeness again that had obviously been drummed into him by a mother who hadn't run off and absconded from the task—shut it, and slid in beside her, starting the engine and pulling out without wasting a moment.

Three minutes later he pulled up outside the patient entrance, reached across and squeezed her hand.

'It'll be OK, Kate,' he murmured.

She wished she had his faith. She wanted to hang onto him but she couldn't. She had to do this bit by herself. Sucking in a deep breath, she pulled her hand away, got out of the car and headed for the entrance without a word.

She couldn't look at him.

That worried him. A lot. She'd obviously spent the whole of yesterday and all of the night fretting herself into a blind panic, and now she'd gone in without him.

He hadn't wanted that, but it was her body; he wasn't in any position to argue with her, so he let her go and tried to steady his breathing. He could feel his heart pounding, the need to be in there—to see his child for what might be the only time—overwhelming him.

His emotions were in turmoil. A child had been the last thing on his wish list since Kerry had died, but now, faced with the reality of it, the existence of a baby in his life assumed mammoth proportions and he couldn't believe how much he wanted it.

He got up, pacing to the window, hands rammed deep in his pockets to stop him from wringing them.

Please call me in. Please, please call me in—
'Mr Ryder?'

His head whipped round, and he strode towards the beckoning sonographer.

'Kate wants you to come in now.'

He nodded, went in and met her eyes. She was lying on the couch, her clothes tucked out of the way so the subtle curve of her abdomen was exposed, and that barely there bump stole his breath away.

He heard the door close behind him, and he crossed the room in a stride and took her hand, uncurling the fingers that were clenching the edge of the couch and wrapping them around his own.

She curled them tight, clinging to him, her eyes searching his.

'I can't look. Can you, please? Just to see if it's all OK?'

Her eyes were frantic, and he could feel the pulse beating in her hand—or was it his? He didn't know. They probably weren't much different.

He nodded, unable to talk, and fixed his eyes on the screen. Kate's lower abdomen was covered in gel already, as if the sonographer had started and then stopped, and as she picked up the wand and moved it over that little curve, a grainy image popped onto the screen.

A baby, very small, but instantly recognisable.

It was lying on its back, its head to the left of the screen, and he could pick out a little tip-tilted nose, the neck and spine running along the underneath of the image, with the faint lines of the ribs across the chest. And within the chest a tiny, tiny heart, beating steadily a zillion times a minute.

His baby's heart.

How had they done this? How had some random act driven by impulse made anything as incredible, as amazing as this? It should have been an act of love, not lust, he thought with a wash of shame.

The wand moved, catching a stubby little hand waving, the teeniest fingers so clear for a moment, and he hauled in a breath and crushed Kate's hand and blinked away the sudden sting of tears.

There was something wrong.

She didn't know what, but his face was rigid, a muscle jumping in his jaw, and she felt dread flood through her.

'What? What's wrong?' she asked, her voice rising with fear, and he shook his head.

'Nothing,' he said, his voice ragged. 'There's nothing wrong. It's just amazing. Look at it, Kate. Please, look at it. It's incredible.'

I can't! I can't see it! How can I make this decision if...?

But her head turned, against her will, and she looked at the grainy screen and gasped.

'Oh—!' She reached out her hand towards the screen, her fingers tracing the line of its nose, coming to rest over the beating heart. And then the tears she couldn't stop slid from the corners of her eyes and she had to blink them away so she could see again. 'It looks so real,' she whispered.

'It is real,' he said gruffly. 'It's real, and it's ours.'

She stared at the little image, registering for the first time the full enormity of what lay ahead, the responsibility, the utter reality of the fact that a tiny, dependent child was growing in her body and she was going to have to nurture and care for it, to guide it, to protect it. To love it, as it deserved to be loved.

And as if to confirm it, the baby waved again, and kicked its legs, the little limbs flickering on the screen as they came and went.

How could she keep it out of danger if she was the biggest threat it faced, either now or in the future? And really, she knew nothing about Sam. Was he a threat as well? Too damaged by grief to take this much responsibility, no matter how good his intentions? What then? Because this wasn't Kerry's baby. Would he resent it, and her, for that?

'Right, I need to take some measurements,' the sonographer said, and talked them through it—the nuchal translucency figure which was the measurement of the fluid between the skin and the back of the baby's neck, which would help determine the likelihood of Down's, the crown to rump measurement so it could be dated—and all the time the baby waved its arms and legs and Kate fell more and more in love and further and further into an abyss of fear and self-doubt.

The sonographer smiled. 'Goodness, what a wriggler! But it's a healthy little foetus, and the nuchal translucency measurement is nice and low. And there's a good strong heartbeat—a hundred and fifty-two a minute. It's all looking good. I'd say you're twelve weeks exactly, which makes it due around the twenty-first of October? Does that fit with your dates?'

They both nodded, and she heard Sam let out

a shaky breath, as if he'd not quite believed until then that it was his.

'Do you want a photo?'

'Yes, please,' they said together.

'Can we have two copies?' Sam asked, and the sonographer nodded.

'Sure. Do you want a different shot?'

'Yeah, why not?' Sam said, his voice gruff.

The second shot was a close-up, showing the baby's head and body, the miniature fingers of one hand, the fine lines of the ribs, and Kate's heart felt swamped with love.

She kissed her fingers, laid them on the screen over the baby's heart, her own breaking.

I can't bear to hurt you...

The sonographer slipped the photos into an envelope and handed it to Sam while Kate stared at the now blank screen.

'There, all done. And I'll see you in eight weeks for the anomaly scan.'

She gave Kate some paper towel to wipe the gel off her tummy, and when it was done she swung her legs over the side and stood up, tucking the little bump away out of sight.

But not out of mind.

Her child was in there, nestled apparently safely in her body, its future in her hands. But they weren't safe hands, they weren't to be trusted. They let everybody down.

I can't do this...

Sam opened the door for her, and Kate walked out of the room, her legs shaking.

So weird.

She'd gone in there a woman, and come out feeling like—a mother?

Was this what a mother felt like? Torn by fear and love and uncertainty for the future? Had her mother felt like this when she'd taken her to school and left her for ever?

'Here.'

She took the envelope Sam was holding out to her with trembling fingers and headed for the door, needing fresh air and space to get her head around the miniature time bomb growing inside her.

Taking her arm as if he knew she needed the support, he led her to the car, opened the door and settled her in, then went round and got in beside her. 'Where to?'

Where? Somewhere a million miles away, so

she didn't have to do this, didn't have to face whatever the future held.

But it wouldn't matter how far she went, she couldn't outrun it.

'Wherever. Just get me out of here, please,' she said, and closed her eyes.

She had no idea where he was taking her. She was beyond caring, beyond noticing, because all she could see was the image of the baby on the screen.

Her baby.

Their baby.

Sam opened her door, and she realised the car had stopped. He helped her out and she followed numbly, crunching over gravel. She could hear the rattle of halliards, the screech of gulls, and they walked past a big boat propped up on some kind of cradle.

The harbour, she thought numbly, and concentrated on putting one foot in front of the other as he led her up the steps onto the sea wall.

'Walk or sit?' he asked, and she shrugged, hugging her arms around herself to try and stop the shaking, but it didn't work and her legs started to give way.

'OK, sit, I think,' he said, catching her before she fell, and he led her to the steps that went down to the sand below. Her legs didn't make it, and she plopped down onto the steps, sagging against him, the emotional roller coaster of the past week and a bit catching up with her all at once, and she turned her head into his shoulder with a little moan.

The feel of his arm around her, the solidity of his body against hers, the reassuring rise and fall of his chest should have soothed her. It didn't. It just reminded her of everything that was at stake, of everything that had happened and wasn't only happening to her.

She ached for peace, but the sea was quiet today, too quiet to soothe her, its power so muted that it wasn't strong enough to override her fear. And maybe it never would be.

'I can't do it, Sam,' she whispered. 'I really can't do it.'

'*We* can, though,' he said, his voice steady and confident. 'Together, we can. And I'll be there for you, Kate, every step of the way. You won't have to do this on your own, I promise.'

His words should have been reassuring. They were meant to be, so why didn't they reassure her?

Because he didn't know her. He didn't know that everyone promised to stand by her and when the chips were down, they all left her. Left, or drove her out.

'You make it sound so easy,' she said bleakly.

'I haven't said it'll be easy. I don't imagine for a moment it'll be easy. That doesn't mean we can't do it, though, if we work together. It's just teamwork, Kate. We're both used to that. We can do it.'

He sounded so *sure.* How? How could he know it would be all right? A few hours at a time in Resus was one thing. This was a lifetime.

She pushed herself upright, shifting away from him, and became aware of another, more pressing matter.

'I need the loo—all that water they made me drink for the scan? Is there one near here?'

He laughed, got to his feet and pulled her up.

'Come on, I'll let you in. We're at James and Connie's house.'

'Oh.' She hung back, wary now. 'Is Connie here? I don't want her to see me.'

'No,' he said, to her relief. 'She's out for the day. You're quite safe, and anyway there's a bathroom in the cabin.'

'Cabin?'

'Yeah, it's in the garden—I'm living in it at the moment. Gives us all elbow room. Come on.'

He was glad Connie was out, too. He wasn't ready yet to explain all this, at least until Kate had made her decision, and he'd realised that her keeping the baby wasn't a foregone conclusion.

He opened the door of the cabin, pointed Kate in the right direction and left her to it, letting himself into the house and putting on the kettle. Technically he had basic cooking facilities in the cabin, but he didn't have any milk and he was sure they wouldn't mind, so he made her a cup of Connie's decaf tea and helped himself to a coffee from the fancy machine that James had installed.

He was watching through the kitchen window when Kate emerged from the cabin.

'I'm up here,' he said, going to the door and looking down at her from the veranda. 'I've made you tea. Sit on the bench there, I'll bring it down.'

The garden would be better than the veranda. More private if anyone wandered past, and she was hanging by a thread. Not that she was alone. So much hinged on today, and if he messed up—

He loaded a tray with their drinks and a packet of gooey cookies he'd found on the side—Connie's, probably, but she'd forgive him—and sat down beside Kate on the bench by the cabin, nursing his mug and giving her time.

She'd left her tea on the tray and was playing with a cookie, breaking bits off and staring down absently at her hands, eating the odd bit but mostly just stalling, he guessed. He let her do it. She'd talk when she was ready.

'I'm sorry,' she said after a long silence that he'd let stretch almost to the limit.

'What for?'

'Being so—cowardly?'

He turned and frowned at her. 'Cowardly?

Having a baby's a big thing, Kate. It's not cowardly to be overwhelmed by it, especially not with your history. Being abandoned as a child is massive, and it's bound to shake your confidence.'

She looked away, but not before he saw the bleak sadness of an old grief in her eyes.

'How could she just leave me, Sam? I must have been a horrible child.'

He had no idea. Her voice was so forlorn that he wanted to kill her mother in that moment. 'Probably no more horrible than any other child,' he said matter-of-factly. 'They all have their special moments, so I don't think you can blame it on yourself. What do you know about her? Do you remember her?'

She shrugged. 'Not really. She used to read to me. I can remember that. I'd snuggle up in bed at night and she'd sit next to me with her arm round me and read. I had a favourite book and she read it to me every night—it was in my school bag that day. She must have put it there. I've still got it.'

The tatty, much loved little book he'd seen on her shelves.

'Is that all you've got of her?' he asked softly, unbearably moved by that because, for all his parents' shortcomings, and they had plenty, he'd always felt secure and loved. And Kate must have done, until that day. 'Just the book?'

She nodded. 'Yes. Social services went to the flat and got my clothes, but there was no trace of her. Her things were there, but she never came back to collect them, so I was told later. She must have walked away with just the clothes she stood up in, but she simply disappeared off the radar and she's never reappeared. Well, not as far as I know. I've never really looked for her, not properly.'

'What about your father?'

She shook her head. 'No father. Social services got a copy of my birth certificate and there was nothing on that, nothing I remember her saying ever, and I don't remember there being any men around, but I was only tiny, don't forget.'

He hadn't forgotten. Not for a second. 'Are you on any social media sites? Might she have seen your name?'

She shook her head. 'No. I don't use my real

name on social media, and I tend to avoid it anyway. I've been burnt.'

He nodded, unsurprised by that. 'I'm glad you're wary of it. The internet can be nasty, and dangerous. Have you tried looking for her at all?'

She nodded. 'A little. There are lots of Rosemary Ashtons, but no one that looks like me. Not that that necessarily means anything, but it's all I've got, that and her name and age and my place of birth. And anyway, I'm not sure I want to see her. I don't know what she'd have to say to me that I might want to hear. It could just make it worse.'

He couldn't see how, but it wasn't his mother, it wasn't his childhood and it wasn't his business, really.

He put his hand over hers and stilled it.

'You're making crumbs,' he said gently, and took the remains of the biscuit out of her hands and put her mug in them. 'Drink up, and we'll go for a walk along the river wall. A leg stretch might clear your head.'

And his, because all he could see was the image of his baby deep within Kate's body, and the tatty little book that was all she had of the mother who'd abandoned her.

He was right, it did clear her head and make her feel better. That, and the tea and cookie, because she'd been too nervous to eat before her scan and her blood sugar must have been in her boots.

They cut across the pub car park and onto the river wall at the harbour mouth, heading behind the boatyard and up along the raised earth bank that held back the river at high tide, and as they strolled she felt the fear fall away a little.

'It's gorgeous here, isn't it?' she said, drawing the air deep into her lungs. 'The way the smell of the river mud takes over from the smell of the sea, the little boats moored out there on the water—it all looks so innocent and peaceful on a day like today with the sun shining and just a light breeze, but it can change so fast. That's what I love about the sea, all that raw power lurking under the surface.'

'Have you ever sailed?'

She laughed. 'When? I lived in London, in a succession of foster homes or children's homes. The longest I was anywhere was five years, and then it all went horribly wrong. Life as a looked-after child isn't a bed of roses, Sam.'

'No, I'm sure it isn't. I'm sorry. I wasn't really implying that. I just wondered if you'd been out in a sailing boat since you'd been here, as you love the sea so much.'

She shook her head. 'No. I don't really know anybody who sails.'

'Well, you do now. When I get the boat fixed, I'll have to take you out in her.'

'Why are they always female?' she asked curiously, strolling along beside him with his arm brushing hers, the slight jostle of it against her anchoring her somehow.

He chuckled. 'I have no idea. It stems from the Mediterranean languages where inanimate objects have a gender, but boats can be a little capricious and unpredictable, so it's probably appropriate.'

'What *are* you saying?' she asked, joining in his laughter, and he slung his arm around her shoulders and hugged her up against his side, flooding her with warmth.

'Present company excepted, of course.' He looked down at her, pausing to brush a swift, light-as-a-feather kiss against her lips. 'Feeling better?'

'Mmm. A bit. It was just a bit of an emotional rollercoaster, really, the scan. Seeing it there, so real—I think I'd been fooling myself, really, until that moment. It hadn't really sunk in.'

'No. I know what you mean. It did make it suddenly very real, didn't it? Real, and utterly amazing. Awe-inspiring, really, the start of a life, of a new, tiny little person. And it's ours, Kate. Some of you, some of me, and yet utterly unique. That's just incredible. The most amazing thing we can ever do in our lives.'

He turned her towards him and cupped her shoulders in his hands, his eyes serious suddenly.

'It will be all right, Kate. Together, we'll make it all right.'

He bent his head, touching his lips to hers again, but slowly this time, a tender, gentle kiss that felt like a promise. Then he drew her up against him and held her there, his chin resting on her head, her ear against his chest so she could hear the steady thud of his heart against his ribs, solid and reassuring.

And somewhere deep inside her, a tiny ember of hope began to flicker into life…

They turned back then, his arm still round her shoulders, his heart feeling lighter because something had happened in that moment when he'd kissed her and held her.

He couldn't define it, but he knew it was there, and it gave him a little more confidence in his ability to pull this off.

'It's just gorgeous here, isn't it?' he murmured as they strolled back up the track towards the cottage. 'The sea on one side, the marshes on the other, but it's this side that's got the best view, especially in the evening with the birds coming in to roost in the reed beds. I could sit on the veranda for hours watching it. I can't imagine why James and Connie want to leave.'

'No, nor can I. If I lived here I don't think I could bring myself to go to work, never mind move!'

He chuckled, then let out a tired sigh. 'I just have to get that blasted boat off the drive so they can sell it. And they went to look at a house yesterday, so the pressure's on a bit.'

She turned her head, following the direction of his gaze, and her eyes widened. 'That's *your* boat? Crumbs. I thought it was much smaller than that! I thought that must be someone else's.'

'Nope. That's the offending article, all twenty-nine feet of her.' They walked up beside it, standing underneath the stern high above them on the cradle, the keel propped on baulks of timber.

'Gosh. I can see what they mean. It's really—'

'An eyesore?'

She laughed softly. 'Well, you said it, but it's not going to set the house off very well, is it, when they try and market it, so what will you do? What *can* you do with it?'

He shrugged. 'Sell it? Move it? I don't know. It all depends if they've got room in the boatyard. Otherwise it'll have to go. I'm sure I can find a buyer.'

'But you really wanted it, Sam.'

'It's just a sentimental attachment to my youth, to a time before everything got too complicated. And I miss sailing.'

'So keep it.'

He gave a short huff of laughter and turned to her, taking her hands in his. 'I want to, but realistically, when the baby comes, what time will I have to work on it? I've said I'll be there for you, and I mean it, Kate. And I'm not just going to pay lip service to it, I intend to be hands-on on a daily basis.'

'If I keep it,' she said, and the bottom dropped out of his stomach.

'Kate—please. Don't do that. Even if you decide you can't cope with motherhood, please, don't do that. Let me bring the baby up. I can do it. I can get help. I'll find a way. Just—please, don't…'

She swallowed hard and looked away.

'I don't know if I could, anyway. Not now I've seen that brave little heart beating.'

'Then don't, because there's no going back. Go through with it, give it and us a chance. Please?'

She hesitated for an age while he held his breath, and then she nodded slowly.

'OK,' she said, and he exhaled sharply and dragged her into his arms, crushing her against his chest.

'Thank you,' he whispered, his voice ragged, his chest heaving with an emotion he couldn't control, and he felt her arms slide round him and hug him back.

He held her for an age, then gradually, as his heart slowed and the world settled back onto an even keel, he released his grip and stood back, staring down into her eyes and smiling.

'Thank you,' he said again, and she bit her lips and blinked hard.

'I can't do it without you, Sam.'

'I know,' he said, his voice firming now. 'I know you can't, but you won't have to.'

'You've said that already.'

'And I meant it, and I'll say it again and again if it helps you to believe in me.'

'I believe in you. It's me I have trouble with.'

'Don't. Don't, because I believe in you. You're a good woman, Kate, and you'll be a good mother.'

'I wish I had your confidence.'

He hugged her again, pressing a kiss to her hair, holding her close. 'It'll come, you'll see.' He looked down into her eyes and smiled. 'I'm starving, and I'm sure you are. Shall we try the pub for lunch?'

'Do they do fish and chips?'

He laughed, the weight of the world suddenly off his shoulders.

'I'm almost certain they do fish and chips,' he said, and, hugging her gently, he wheeled them round and headed back towards the pub.

CHAPTER SIX

THE PUB HADN'T started serving lunch when they got there, so they sat outside in the unseasonably lovely sunshine, sipping fizzy water with ice and lemon and watching the world go by.

There were children crabbing off the little jetty by the ferry, an elderly couple sharing a pot of mussels from the hut, the odd car coming or going from the boatyard, but it was still early in the season so for the most part they were on their own.

Kate turned her face up to the sun, listened to the keening of the gulls and felt the tension inside her ease a little.

'It's so peaceful here. My flat's right in the thick of it—I can hear the ambulance sirens going, the drone of traffic, the dogs over the road barking constantly, people yelling to each other and laughing when they come out of the pubs—sometimes it's hard to get to sleep it's so noisy. And it doesn't help that it's just single glazed, with that thin old Victorian glass and rattling sash windows that let in every bit of passing breeze.'

He laughed, his eyes crinkling with wry amusement. 'You're really selling it to me,' he said drily. 'Considering I was going to suggest that I move in with you, you might need to do a better job.'

She stared at him, slightly taken aback by that coming out of nowhere. 'You want to move in?'

His brows pleated. 'Well—yes. If we're going to do this together, don't you think we should start as we mean to go on? It's not as if we need to take it slow in case it doesn't work. We *have* to make it work. We have to build trust, and learn to compromise and accommodate each other's needs. And no, it probably won't be easy, but it's going to have to happen if we want to make this work, and it's better we do it before the baby comes.'

She could feel her heart racing, fluttering against her ribs like a caged bird. 'Oh. I thought we'd do that after I have the baby.'

'Why wait? Since it's going to happen, why not just get on with it?'

Because she wasn't ready? Because she wasn't sure she could keep her emotional distance from him and preserve what was left of her sanity if he was there all the time, day and night, by her side?

'I'm not sleeping with you,' she said bluntly. 'Not until I'm sure it's working.'

He let out a soft huff of laughter. 'That again? And I haven't asked you to, Kate, but it's up to you. It's not exactly unprecedented, it's how we ended up where we are now, but if that's where it took us...'

She felt his hand cover hers, pick it up, turn it over. Felt the soft graze of stubble, the touch of his lips against her palm, and his fingers folding hers up, closing them over the kiss as if to keep it safe.

'Would it be so bad?' he asked, and she felt her pulse quicken.

Bad? Hardly. But—sensible?

She retrieved her hand, folded it in her lap with the other one to keep it out of trouble. 'No, of course not, but that doesn't make it a good idea.

Not until we're sure we can make it work—and I
have warned you, I'm a nightmare to live with.'

She felt him sigh. 'Maybe you're right, maybe
we should take it slow. There's no hurry, after
all.'

She felt the sink of disappointment, and told
herself not to be ridiculous.

'I just—I don't think we should take anything
for granted. I want to tread carefully, not make
any more mistakes. My life's littered with them,
and yes, it would be amazing if we got on and
it was all dead easy and we can live together
in blissful harmony, but I gave up believing in
happy ever after a long time ago, Sam, and I still
can't really believe we're actually going through
with it.'

'No, nor can I, but I can't tell you how relieved
I am that we are. I know that must have taken a
lot of courage.'

She shook her head slowly. 'I was just scared,
Sam. I *am* scared. I was only thinking about pro-
tecting the baby from the hell I went through as
a child. I couldn't bear that on my conscience.'

A tear trickled down her cheek, and he wiped
it gently away with his thumb. 'You won't have

it on your conscience, Kate, because there's no way that's going to happen to our baby, I promise. It's going to have a stable home, with two parents who love it and care for it. And, yes, things will go wrong from time to time, and it will be hurt, but that's life, and life hurts. Even when it's perfect, it can hurt. It can hurt like hell. But you get up, and you dust yourself off, and you move on and find a new way forward. And that's what we have to do, starting right now. And learning how to share a home is a good first step.'

She looked at him, at those magnetic blue eyes, so serious now, so intent, so focused on keeping her and her baby safe, and she nodded and leant in to kiss him.

It was a chaste kiss, not quite fleeting but not lingering either, and before she gave in to temptation she pulled away again and smiled wryly.

'Can we have lunch first, before you move in? I'm starving.'

After a startled second he began to laugh, and slinging his arm round her shoulders, he hugged her close. 'Yes, you crazy girl, we can have lunch first. And there's no hurry, I can stay with James and Connie as long as I want. Come on, let's go in and find a table by the window. I know you like something other than me to look at.'

It wasn't true. She could look at him all day without getting bored, but she wasn't going to tell him that. Not if their idea of a hands-off getting-to-know-each-other period was going to stand the vaguest chance of working. And as her lips were still tingling from the most innocent kiss on record, she was pretty sure the idea was doomed.

He caught James on the way in that evening.

He'd dropped Kate home because she said she needed to go shopping, and he'd spent an hour or two on the boat to keep himself busy so Connie wouldn't be tempted to waylay him with coffee when she got back, but she just smiled up at him, the baby on her hip, the dog sniffing round the bottom of the ladder in the curls of stripped-off old paint, and told him to crack on.

'Just so you know, we want that house we saw yesterday and the agent's coming tomorrow to value this one, so I'm really going to have to nag you about that heap,' she said cheerfully, and he went back to the paint stripping without bothering to tell her that there wasn't a hope in hell of him getting the boat finished and off the drive for months, let alone the sort of timeframe she had in mind.

He was still up the ladder two hours later when James pulled his car in across the back of Connie's, and he turned off the blowtorch and climbed down.

'Nice to see you hard at work, but don't stop on my account,' James said, giving the boat a jaundiced look.

He gave James a wry grin. '*Et tu, Brute?* Look, are you in later this evening? There's something I need to talk to you about.'

'Yes, of course. We want to talk to you, too. Join us for dinner?'

'No, thanks, Kate's cooking,' he said, wondering what it was they wanted to talk about. The boat, probably. Almost inevitably. 'I was thinking of later, after you've put Joseph to bed and finished eating. And I'd like to bring Kate, if that's OK.'

James opened his mouth, scanned Sam's face and shut it.

'Eight thirty? We should be done by then.'

Sam nodded, cleared up the tools and headed for the shower. He wasn't looking forward to this, but as his boss as well as a friend, James had to know what was going on. Whatever James and Connie wanted to say to him, it couldn't be as significant as his news. He just hoped they could get over it and add their support.

The shops were useless. Nobody seemed to stock maternity clothes, so she bought some underwear and a couple of long, floaty tops that might gloss over the problem for a little while at least, and went to see Annie.

She'd had yet another missed call from her during the morning while her phone had been switched off, and as she pulled onto the drive she saw her through the window, sitting in a chair with her feet up and the girls playing quietly on the floor.

She waved to them, and the girls squealed and ran to the front door, all but dragging her inside. She let them tow her into the sitting room, Chloe on one side, Grace on the other, and she smiled at Annie over their excited chatter.

'Hello, stranger,' she said softly. 'I haven't seen you for over a week. How are you?'

Kate shrugged, suddenly lost for words. There was so much she wanted to say, to ask, so much she couldn't say in front of the children, and Annie tutted and got awkwardly to her still-swollen feet.

'Are we going to have cake?' Chloe asked hopefully.

'I'm going to get us a cup of tea. If you're good and stay in here and play nicely, I might let you have some. Can you do that?'

'Yes, Mummy,' they chorused, and Annie rolled her eyes.

'Works like a charm,' she said drily. 'Come on, let's go and have five minutes' peace while the kettle boils.' And she propelled Kate out of the sitting room and into the kitchen, shutting the door firmly.

'OK, what's up? I've been worrying about you all weekend. Why didn't you ring me or answer my calls?'

'I didn't know what to say. It's been a bit momentous,' she said, knowing it was the understatement of the year. 'I had my scan,' she added, and pulled the envelope out of her bag.

Annie took it without opening it and met her eyes searchingly. 'Are you OK?'

'I think so. I'm still trying to get my head round it. Well, we both are.'

'Both?' Her eyes widened. 'Are you talking about the father? I thought you didn't have his contact details? Did you manage to find him?'

She tried to smile. 'Yes—or rather, he found me, by accident. It turns out he's actually Connie's friend. Your locum?'

'The guy with the boat?' Annie's jaw dropped, and she recovered herself after a second and shook her head. 'Wow. So how did you meet him?'

'In a bar. He stayed an extra night to see the boat, I was supposed to meet Petra but she didn't make it, and—well, I don't know, he was just there, and…'

'Oh, Kate,' Annie sighed. 'So how is he about it?'

'Not thrilled, but actually he's been amazing, really, considering. He's talked me into keeping it, telling me I can do it, and he even said if

I couldn't cope, he'd bring the baby up himself on his own.'

'Gosh. That sounds almost too good to be true.'

'That's because it is. His fiancée died two years ago, just before their wedding, and this is just so far off his radar, but he's determined that we can do it together. I just hope he's right because I honestly don't think I can do it without him, and even with him will be hard enough.'

'Wow,' Annie said again. 'Poor guy. But at least he's taken responsibility for it and you're not going to be alone.'

'No, but he wants to move in, and I'm not sure I can cope with it, Annie. What if he finds he *can't* do it? It'll be so much worse if we've been living together like a couple. We'll have so much more invested in it—not that we can have much more than sharing a child, but even so…'

'Does he have a name?'

She laughed. 'Yes, he has a name. Sam—Sam Ryder.'

'Nice name. Good, strong name. Good-looking, of course?'

Her smile was wry. 'Very. He's a proper hottie.'

Annie shook her head. 'Well, I have to say, Kate, if you had to make a mistake, he sounds like a good one. He's a doctor, he's single, he's being supportive—realistically, could you ask for more?'

She swallowed. 'Him not to be stuck with me against his will? Not to be making the best of a situation he really, really doesn't want to be in? Him to love me? He's a really, really nice man, Annie, and under any other circumstances he'd be a real catch, but I can't compete with his dead fiancée, I just can't...'

Her eyes flooded, and Annie put her arms round her and hugged her.

'Give him time. He'll get over her, and this is so new to both of you—you'll work it out.'

'Oh, Annie, I hope so.' She pulled away and sniffed. 'What about that tea? Shall I put the kettle on while you get the cake out for the girls?'

'Don't you want some?'

Kate laughed sadly. 'You know me too well, but I shouldn't, really. Nothing fits me any more as it is.'

'Don't buy any maternity clothes! I'm never going to need them again, and I'll have lots of baby clothes I can hand on as they grow out of them. Really, you don't need to get anything, Kate, unless you want to.'

'Oh, Annie, thank you,' she said, and her eyes welled again. 'I still can't really believe it's happening.'

Annie picked up the scan photo envelope and waggled it at her. 'Really?' She eased them out of the envelope and studied them for a moment, her face softening. 'They're lovely photos,' she said quietly. 'Sometimes they're just in the wrong position and they can't get a decent image, but these are perfect.'

'It waved,' she said, and nearly set herself off again, and Annie put the photos back in the envelope, handed it to her and got out the mugs.

'Come on, you. Cup of tea, slice of Marnie's cake—chocolate this week—and then we'll go and look at my clothes. And then at some point in the not too distant future, I'd like to meet this man of yours.'

She cooked for Sam that night—nothing huge after the fish and chips they'd had in the pub, just a stir fry with noodles, but she managed not to ruin it, which felt like progress.

'I spoke to James,' he told her as she dished up. 'We're going round there at eight thirty. They're going to want to know why I'm moving out and they don't need to hear stuff on the grapevine. I thought it would be best to get it over with.'

She nodded. 'Yes, I suppose so. I told Annie today that you're the father. She was really sweet—and she wants to meet you. She's offered me lots of stuff—maternity clothes and baby things. She says I can have all the clothes as the boys grow out of them.'

'What if it's a girl?'

She smiled. 'She probably won't mind the odd blue thing.'

'I'm sure we can find some pretty pink stuff if the need arises. Do you mind what it is?'

Her hands strayed instinctively to her tummy, surprised yet again by the little bump that seemed to be growing by the hour. 'No—no, I don't think so. I just want it to be happy. It's the only thing that matters—'

He reached out and squeezed her hand. 'It will be. We'll make sure of it. This smells good,' he added, picking up his fork and digging in. 'Mmm. Tasty,' he mumbled, and she felt a ridiculous surge of pride.

'So, when are you planning on moving in?' she asked, going back to their earlier conversation.

'Whenever. I haven't got a lot of stuff. We could do it in one car load.'

'Oh. OK. What do you think they'll say?' she asked. 'About the baby, I mean.'

'James—probably not a lot. It'll be Connie that has the opinion, I would imagine. Whatever, it's our baby, Kate, not theirs, and at the end of the day it doesn't really matter what they feel about it, but I like to think they'll be supportive.'

Kate wasn't so sure, and her heart was pounding a little as they pulled up outside on the dot of eight thirty.

'OK?' Sam asked her, pausing on the veranda before knocking, and she nodded.

She wasn't, but it had to be done. 'OK,' she lied, and tried to smile, but she was too nervous and if it wasn't for the fact that they were Sam's friends, she would have legged it.

'It'll be fine,' he said softly, stroking his knuckles over her cheek in a gentle gesture of reassurance.

'I doubt it.' She heard scratching at the door and the handle rattle, and his hand fell away as James opened the door, his hand firmly in Saffy's collar.

'Come on in. Connie's in the sitting room. Kate, are you all right with the dog or shall I shut her away?'

'No, I'm fine with her,' she said, fondling Saffy's ears, and she was rewarded by a thrashing tail and a cheerful, lolling tongue that reminded her of her foster parents' dogs. They'd been a refuge for her when things had turned sour, and she'd missed them ever since.

She followed Sam through the kitchen and round through a wide opening into a lovely, cosy room, with a pair of sofas facing each other across an old leather trunk that doubled as a coffee table and, beyond them, framed by a huge bay window, was a spectacular view of the sea.

The light was fading now, a pale band on the distant horizon all that was left of the day, and Connie switched on the table lamps as they went in, banishing the dusk and flooding the room with warmth.

'Hello, Kate, how are you? I haven't seen you for ages. Are you OK?' she asked, and Kate nodded, wishing the ground could open up and swallow her. These were her colleagues, people she'd worked with, people who'd seen her at her best and worst.

And this, she thought grimly, was definitely her worst. She pasted a smile firmly on her face and mentally battened down the hatches. 'I'm fine. How are you?'

'Blooming. I love being pregnant,' Connie said, her happy smile just underlining the difference in their circumstances. 'Can I get you a drink? Glass of wine? Cup of coffee?'

What could she say to that that wouldn't give the game away? Not that Sam wasn't just about to, but even so…

'Actually, have you got any sparkling water?'

'Yes, sure. Sam?'

'I'll have coffee, Connie, please.'

She went into the kitchen, leaving Sam crouched down rubbing Saffy's tummy, and Kate stood in the bay window watching the rapidly fading light and wondering what it would be like to live in a house like this. She'd never been in it before, but it was love at first sight, and she couldn't imagine how James and Connie could even consider leaving it.

'So, what was it you wanted to talk to me about?' Sam asked as Connie and James came out of the kitchen.

'Oh, no, you first,' Connie said, putting the tray of drinks down on the old trunk, and Kate's heart gave a thump.

James waved at a sofa. 'Kate, Sam, sit down, make yourselves at home.'

There wasn't really a prayer of that, but as she didn't have much alternative she perched on the nearest sofa. Connie plonked herself down on the other sofa next to James, with the result that she and Sam ended up facing them across the trunk. It felt as if they were being interviewed, and she was glad when Saffy came and leant against her legs so she could stroke her to give her hands something to do apart from shake.

'So, come on then, what is it?' Connie prompted, and beside her Kate felt Sam haul in a deep breath before pulling one of the scan photos out of his jacket pocket and dropping it on the trunk in front of them.

'We're having a baby,' he said quietly, and Kate held her breath in the stunned silence that followed.

To her surprise Connie's eyes filled with tears as she picked up the photo and stared at it. 'How? You haven't had time…'

'It doesn't take long, and I would imagine you know *how*, so I won't elaborate,' Sam said drily. 'We met in January, the night I stayed on to see the boat.'

'Well, I know that, but I hadn't realised you'd…'

She trailed off, and he nodded. 'And that's it, really. There isn't a lot more I can add.'

Connie let her breath out on a shaky sigh and put the photo down. 'Oh, Sam. Are you OK?' she asked, her voice gentle, as if she knew he wasn't.

'We're working on it,' he said quietly, and Connie glanced across at Kate.

Until then her focus had been on Sam, all her concern for him, but that was natural. He was her friend, and he'd been through hell recently.

She and Connie weren't much more than acquaintances, so she didn't expect any sympathy, but now Connie's eyes were on her and she realised she'd been wrong about that.

'Kate?' she asked softly.

Kate shrugged. 'You know me, Connie, one disaster after another,' she said lightly, trying to get the quiver out of her voice. 'I mess everything up. It seems to be my job in life to ruin other people's, never mind my own—'

'No!' Sam's voice was firm. 'It was an accident, Kate, and at the end of the day it was my fault, not yours, so don't go taking all the blame.'

'But it *was* my fault! If I'd taken the morning-after pill—'

'You were sick, it would've been too late, and anyway, you shouldn't have needed to—'

'Whoa,' James said, chipping in for the first time. 'You two really are having a guilt fest, aren't you?'

Sam sucked in a breath and let it out in a rush. 'Sorry, we're a bit fraught. It's been a tough day for both of us at the end of a difficult week, but we just wanted you to know the situation.'

Sam's hand found hers, enclosing it in a reassuring grip, and she leant against him, grateful for his solid warmth in the turbulent sea of emotions that filled the room. As if to reinforce the comfort, she felt Saffy lick her hand, and she stroked the warm, silky head that lay across her knees.

'Will you be really all right?' Connie asked. 'It's so soon—you don't even know each other. What are you going to do?'

'We're keeping it,' he said calmly, although Kate was sure he was anything but calm. 'Together. I'm going to move into Kate's flat, and we'll work it out as we go along.'

Kate felt Connie's eyes on her and looked up to see concern flare in them, but who it was for she couldn't tell. Any one of the three involved, the baby included, would have been a suitable candidate.

'Kate?'

She tried to smile, but it was a pretty poor effort so she gave up and shrugged. 'We have to start somewhere. Now is as good a time as any. We've only got six months before the baby comes, and we need to—how was it you put it?'

she asked, turning to Sam. 'Find a new way forward? Especially Sam.'

'No,' he said firmly. 'This is just as hard for you, if not harder. It's a no-brainer for me to keep the baby. It's taking much more courage for you to do it.'

That was news to her. She'd felt it was him who was struggling the most, him who was finding it so hard because of his grief, because of Kerry. She was just plain terrified and convinced it was doomed to failure like every other relationship, but he seemed to have understood the depth of her fears, and just that simple fact suddenly made it all seem so much easier.

'So—you're really going to live in the flat?' Connie asked. 'Up all those stairs with a baby and a buggy and all the shopping? You live on the top floor, don't you, Kate?'

'Yes, but it's fine—'

'It'll be fine for now, but we'll sort out something a bit more permanent when we know where I'm going to be working next,' Sam said, and she felt a little stab of unease.

She knew her flat wasn't great, but it was her home, and although at times it was lonely, it was hers, nobody could tell her what to do in it, and suddenly that all felt threatened. Especially the possibility of moving away from all her friends...

'Actually, you may not have to go anywhere,' James said, stopping her thoughts in their tracks. 'I've got a feeling Annie won't come back after her maternity leave, and if the job comes up, we'll need to replace her. Would a part-time consultancy be enough for you?'

Sam shrugged thoughtfully. 'Maybe, if the contract was right. It would give me time to bond with the baby, and to be near our friends would be a massive bonus for both of us.'

'The job's not set in stone,' James warned him. 'But we already need more consultant cover than we have at the moment, so I might be able to do something anyway. Would that tempt you enough?'

It would, he realised. It did.

He turned to Kate, searching her face. 'How would you feel about that?'

'Staying here, near my friends?' Her face seemed to light up from within, and he felt a pang of guilt that he'd even contemplated taking her away from them. 'It would be amazing. I really don't want to leave—'

'It's not a firm job offer,' James reminded them. 'Not yet, anyway, and you'd have to be interviewed, of course, but getting people of your calibre is extremely hard so there's a definite possibility I could talk the board into offering you a full-time senior consultant's post, especially if Annie does leave. Just bear it in mind.'

He nodded, his heart suddenly beating a little faster, the prospect more appealing than he could possibly have imagined. To be here, near his own friends, near the sea...

'Leaving that on one side for a moment, it's high time we said congratulations about the baby. I know it won't be easy, but you're both determined enough to make this work. I hope you'll be very happy together.'

Sam swallowed hard, trying desperately not to think of the last time he'd heard those words—his engagement to Kerry.

'Thanks,' he said gruffly. 'We'll give it our best shot.'

He put his arm round Kate, hugged her to his

side and dropped a kiss on her cheek. She smiled, curled her fingers over his jaw and kissed him back, and her warmth flowed into him, easing the sadness.

Maybe it will work, he thought. Maybe...

'So, having got that out of the way, what was it you two wanted to talk to me about?'

James gave a slightly awkward laugh, and met Connie's eyes.

'You, or me?'

'It's the boat, Sam,' Connie said tentatively.

He sighed. 'I thought as much.'

'I know it's not a good time to hassle you,' James cut in, taking over, 'but we need to move fast on this, if we want the house we saw yesterday. They've had other offers, lower ones, but we're not in a strong position unless we've got a buyer, and we don't need anything that's going to put someone off, and we're very afraid the boat will.'

Sam nodded slowly. 'Look, I'll talk to the guy in the boatyard about moving it. How long have I got?'

James sighed. 'Someone wants to view it tomorrow. They haven't even seen the details, but the agent sounded them out and they seem keen. And we know you can't move it by then, but if we could at least tell them it was going…?'

'Or you could always buy the house yourself, Sam,' Connie said with a laugh. 'That would solve it at a stroke.'

There was a stunned silence, and he turned and looked at Kate. 'Fancy living here?'

He saw her jaw sag slightly.

'I think Connie's joking,' she said, before he could talk himself into it. 'And anyway, you haven't got a job yet.'

'I *was* joking,' Connie chipped in. 'Seriously, I don't expect you to buy the house, Sam. That would be crazy!'

He gave a wry smile and sat back. 'Yeah, you're probably right,' he murmured, and mentally put the idea on the back burner. 'So, tell us all about this new house that you want.'

CHAPTER SEVEN

THEY LEFT A short while later, but not before Connie got in a parting shot.

'Let us know how you get on with the boat-yard,' she said, a weeny bit pointedly, but Sam just grinned at her.

'You're a nag, do you know that?'

As he slid behind the wheel and started the engine, he glanced across at Kate and said, 'So how *would* you feel about living there?'

She felt her heart lurch. 'Really? It would be amazing, but it's never going to happen so I don't really want to think about it.'

'What if it could happen?'

She turned so she could see him better, but the interior light was out by then and the night closed in around them as he drove off, so her only clue was his voice.

And that was giving nothing away.

'How? Where are you going to find the money?

Because I haven't got any—well, not that would make any difference.'

'I've got a house. Kerry and I bought it, but we never lived in it. We were going to move in after the wedding, but—whatever, it was furnished, ready to go, so I just contacted a letting agent. I'm sure he could sell it for me.'

'You can't do that!' she said, shocked that he would even consider it when it had so much meaning for him, but he just shrugged.

'Why not? I've never set foot in it. It means nothing to me, I only ever saw it on plan, but the tenants have wanted to buy it since the word go, and it's risen hugely in value. I could sell it to them.'

His voice was still emotionless, so she could only presume that it really did mean nothing to him. Either that or he was better than she thought at hiding his feelings.

'You still don't have a permanent job, though, so you don't even know how long you'll be in Yoxburgh.'

'No, but I'm here for a year, Annie's told James that much, and I don't suppose their house would be hard to sell, not with that view. And he was dangling the carrot of a pretty decent job firmly in front of my nose. He wouldn't do that if he didn't think it was possible. So—should I see if the tenants still want it?'

Kate let out a long, slow breath. 'Sam, it's a huge thing to do, to give up your house like that—'

'No. It's not huge, Kate, it's just a house, and I don't even have a mortgage on it. The life insurance covered it, so it was paid off in full. It's just an investment, nothing more.'

She wasn't convinced, but then nothing about their relationship was without drawbacks or compromise on both sides.

'Don't you think we should find out if we can actually live together without killing each other before you do anything radical?' she asked, trying hard to be sensible in the face of his overconfidence and her own self-doubts, but he just laughed softly and reached out a hand and found hers.

'We'll be fine,' he said, threading his fingers through hers and giving them a little squeeze, and she felt a little of his confidence seep into her along with the warmth.

He pulled up outside her house, and she took off her seat belt and turned to him, searching his face in the dim light from the streetlamps.

'Fancy a coffee?'

He hesitated, then shook his head, the engine still running. 'No, better not, we've both got an early start.'

She nodded, then leant across and touched her lips to his.

'I'll see you tomorrow, then,' she said, moving away, but before she could go far his hand reached out and eased her back towards him. He met her halfway, his lips grazing hers, questioning, tasting, sipping, until on a slow, soft outbreath he moved in closer, deepening the kiss, exploring her mouth until she whimpered.

The needy sound was enough to make him go still and pull away, to her regret, but he didn't go far—just enough to rest his forehead against hers and let out a ragged sigh.

'Sorry, I didn't mean to do that. You'd better go in while I'll still let you,' he said gruffly after a long pause, and she nodded, pulled away reluctantly and opened the door.

'Goodnight, Sam. I'll see you tomorrow.'

'Yeah. Sleep well.'

'And you.' She shut the car door, ran up to her flat and waved to him from the window. He lifted a hand, then drove away, and she rested her head against the cool glass and swallowed hard.

OK, so maybe they wouldn't kill each other if they lived together, but hands off? Not a chance. Not while her body was burning up from that brief but thorough kiss, and she had a feeling he wasn't doing any better.

He contacted the letting agent in the morning, then rang the boatyard—just in case.

'Any joy?'

'Do you usually eavesdrop on people's conversations?' he asked mildly, and James just chuckled.

'You're talking on the phone in the middle of the ED in a very unnerving quiet spell, and you're worried about me eavesdropping?'

He slid his phone back into his pocket and ignored that. 'In answer to your first question, not yet. They certainly can't move the boat today, but I'm serious about the house.'

James frowned in surprise. 'Really? I thought you were just being silly.'

'No. I'd love it. It's got everything we need. Why wouldn't I want it?'

'I don't know. Come on, let's move this into my office and we can have a proper conversation about it.'

They'd taken two steps when the red phone rang, and James rolled his eyes.

'I thought it was too quiet. We'll catch up later.'

The trauma call went out on the loudspeakers as he was talking.

'Adult trauma call, five minutes. Paediatric trauma call, five minutes. Adult trauma call, ten minutes.'

James pulled out his phone. 'I've got to make a quick call and then I'll meet you in Resus. Can you pull together a couple of teams?'

'Sure.' He turned on his heel and nearly ran into Kate. He hadn't seen her all morning, she'd been in Minors, but the kiss was fresh in his mind and he'd had to force himself to focus.

'Are you free?'

'Yes. Do you want me?'

He gave a wry, frustrated chuckle. 'Can we talk about that after we've taken the trauma call?'

She coloured slightly, bit her lips and tried not to laugh. 'I'll take that as a yes, then,' she said, and he picked up the information from the desk and followed her into Resus where the teams were already waiting.

'OK, we've got two adults and a baby all from the same car,' he told them. 'Dad's still being cut out, mum and baby will be here in a minute. I'll do the primary surveys while we wait for James, and we'll go from there. Is someone coming down from Paeds?'

'Not sure. Ed Shackleton's gone off,' someone said, 'so they're trying to find his registrar.'

'OK. Right, we're on. Let's go and meet them.'

The paramedics wheeled the mother in, the screaming baby strapped safely in an infant carrier.

'Mother and five month old infant, vehicle in collision with a van which swerved across the road out of control. We've secured the spine, but she's complaining of abdominal pain and there's evidence of seat belt injuries. BP one-thirty over eighty, pulse one-twenty, GCS fifteen at the scene. The baby's stable but we haven't taken her out of the carrier. Father on his way in with leg injuries.'

Sam nodded, and then turned to Kate. 'Can you get her on a monitor, please, and we need to get some pictures of that spine. I just want to make sure the baby's OK.'

He checked it quickly, one ear on Kate's re-assuring voice as she talked to the mother. She was on a spinal board with a neck brace and she was coherent, but he needed to check her over, too, and the baby seemed fine and was moving normally and the cry was one of distress rather than pain.

'OK, little one, let's see how Mum is, shall we?' he murmured, and went over to her bed, leaving the baby still in her carrier in the care of a nurse until Ed's registrar came down.

Agitated, was the simple answer. 'I need to be with Evie!' she said, trying to get off the trolley, but Kate restrained her gently.

'She's in good hands, Jenny, and so are you. This is Sam. He's one of our consultants and he's going to be looking after you so let's get you checked over quickly and we'll do our best to get you back with her.'

'Hi, Jenny,' Sam chipped in, running his eyes over her carefully after scanning the monitor. 'Evie's fine, from what I can see, but I need to have a look at you now. Can you tell me where you hurt?'

'Uh—my shoulder? My hip—where the seat belt was. And sort of under my ribs?'

'OK, can we cut these clothes off, please, so I can get a proper look, and can we have portable X-rays, please?'

Kate cut them away and he palpated her carefully, but even so she gasped as he touched the area over her liver, and he looked up at Kate.

'Can we do a FAST scan and get a line in, please?' he said softly. 'I just want to check for free fluids. And we'd better get four units of O-neg down here and cross-match for four more. She might have an encapsulated bleed, or it could just be bruising from the seat belt or maybe a fractured rib.'

'I'm on it,' Kate said, and Sam took charge of the ultrasound while she dealt with the bloods.

They moved quickly, and by the time her husband was wheeled in, Sam had established that she had a broken rib, but there was no free fluid, the monitor was tracking a steady blood pressure and her spine and pelvis were uninjured, so Kate could remove the brace.

But in the meantime the baby was still crying, and Sam looked up at Kate and made a decision he hoped he wouldn't regret.

'Can you help me with the baby? I don't know where Paeds are, but I want to get her out and check her over properly.'

She nodded and bent over the mother. 'Jenny, we're just going to look at Evie again. We'll do it right here, next to you, OK, so you can see her?'

Jenny nodded, and he undid the straps on the baby carrier and slid his hands round under the baby. 'You take her head, and we'll lift her on your count,' he said, and they laid her gently down on the bed so he could examine her.

'I want to roll her to check her back. Can you try and keep her head still and in line, please, while we do it? That's lovely.'

She held the baby rock-steady, talking soothingly all the time as he felt carefully for anything untoward, but there was nothing and as he rolled her back and refastened her nappy, Evie lifted her arms and wailed pathetically.

'Can I?' Kate pleaded, and he nodded.

'She's fine. Go for it.'

He watched her stoop and lift the little girl tenderly into her arms, and had to swallow a lump in his throat.

'There, there, sweet thing, it's all right,' she crooned, 'you're OK. Come on, now—there, that's better.' She was rocking gently from foot to foot, cradling little Evie against her shoulder as if she'd done it a million times before, and the baby's wails faded to hiccupping little sobs as she snuggled into the comfort of Kate's shoulder.

He eased his breath out on a sigh and met her eyes. 'There you go,' he said, his voice a little gruff. 'You're a natural. She just needed a little cuddle.'

Kate bent her head and pressed her lips gently to the baby's soft, downy curls and smiled at him, and he felt something he hadn't known was tight release inside his chest.

An hour later all three of them were out of Resus, the father to Theatre, the little girl to Paediatric ICU for monitoring, her mother in a wheel-chair by her side after a clear CT scan, and Sam flashed Kate a smile that made her heart beat faster.

'Good job. Thank you,' he said, and she felt a little rush of warmth.

'You're welcome. Have we got time for a coffee?'

'I hope so. I haven't had lunch yet, either, and it's nearly two. Grab a sandwich together?'

She nodded, and they headed for the canteen, just as Sam's phone buzzed.

'Ah, text from the letting agent. The tenants still want the house.' He shot her a quick glance. 'I am serious, Kate,' he said softly. 'I do want this, but only if you do, too.'

She felt the usual rush of conflicting emotions—hope, excitement even, and the dreaded 'what-ifs'.

What if we can't live together? What if he can't stand the sight of me by the time the baby's born? What if something goes wrong with the pregnancy and I lose it—?

She gave a little gasp, her hand flying to her tiny bump, and Sam stopped.

'What? What is it?'

She shook her head. 'Nothing. I was just thinking—Sam, if you buy the house and I lose the baby—'

'You won't lose it.'

'You can't say that! I might! It happens. And then what?'

He let go of her elbow and turned back towards the canteen. 'You won't,' he said again, as if he was trying to convince himself.

'You sound like King Canute. Fight the battles you can win, Sam. That isn't one of them. If it happens, it happens, and then you'll have another house you won't want to live in.'

'It's still a good house,' he said, when they'd paid for their drinks and sandwiches, and she let out a little sigh and headed for the benches outside.

'Yes. Yes, it is still a good house. It's a lovely house, you're right, and you wouldn't have any trouble selling it on.'

'Have you ever looked round it?'

'No. That was the first time I'd been inside. I'm not really friends with them, Sam, but I don't need to see any more to know it's wonderful.'

'Why don't I ask James if you can have a look round tonight?'

'Because they've got someone else viewing it,' she reminded him.

'Even better, it'll be tidy. And talk of the devil,' he said with a grin as James came over to them. 'We want to look at the house tonight.'

James perched on the arm of the bench and shook his head slowly. 'Sam, I can't promise you a job yet—'

'You don't need to. I've got one for a year—'

'No. You've got one until Annie comes back. If anything goes wrong she's still entitled to her full maternity leave, but she might not want to take it. And safe pregnancy isn't a certainty.'

'You two are full of gloom and doom today. Kate was just talking about that with our baby.'

Our baby.

The words seem to trip off his tongue so easily, and she found them so hard to say. So hard to believe, to comprehend the full implications of those two little words, but her arms had felt so empty when she handed Evie over to the paediatric team and she could only imagine how

Jenny had felt while she'd lain there helpless with Evie crying.

Her phone jiggled in her pocket, and she pulled it out and felt her heart sink. 'They must have heard us talking. Annie's been admitted. Her blood pressure went up and they're doing her C-section today. Oh, lord, I hope she's all right. That must be where Ed was. I wondered.'

'How many weeks is she now?' Sam asked.

'Thirty-four? Not enough.'

'That should be OK, though.'

'Whatever, I'm crossing my fingers, just in case,' Kate said, tapping in a reply. 'Poor Annie. She so badly wanted to get to thirty-five weeks, if not more, but when I saw her yesterday she seemed tired.'

'Not as tired as she's going to be,' James said with a wry laugh. 'I couldn't believe how tired we were with just *one* baby. Right, back to work. Keep us posted.'

It was hard to concentrate for the rest of her shift, and by the time she went off at four she was really twitchy.

She'd been checking her phone all afternoon,

and she was halfway home when it pinged and she pulled it out of her pocket to see a text from Ed, a picture of a smiling Annie cradling two tiny, perfect babies in her arms. She turned round, went back to the hospital, showed it to Sam and James and burst into tears.

'Hey, come on, they're all OK, that's good news,' Sam said, hugging her, and she nodded furiously and sniffed.

'I know, but they lost a baby before they got married and it's just so lovely for them…'

She welled up again, and Sam put his arm round her shoulders and hugged her again, then tilted her chin up so she met his eyes. 'Go and see her,' he said.

'She won't want me. She'll be tired, and the girls will want to see her, and her mum, and Ed's grandmother—she won't want me.'

'Of course she will. Just pop up—five minutes, that's all, not even that. Just to give her a hug. It'll mean a lot.'

Trust Sam to understand. Apart from when he was trying unsuccessfully to stick to their hands-off rule, he was a very tactile person, and so was Annie. She nodded and headed for Maternity.

Annie was alone when she got there, and for a second Kate thought she was asleep, but then she stirred and opened her eyes and her face lit up. 'Kate—you came! Did you get Ed's text?'

'I did—they look gorgeous,' she said, stooping to hug her and blinking back tears. 'You must be so happy. Are you all right?'

'I'm fine—still numb at the moment so everything's peachy! The babies are in SCBU for the night, just to make sure everything's OK, but they're looking great, really strong and feisty, and I'm feeling better already now I know the babies are OK.'

She caught hold of Kate's hand. 'Sit down, talk to me.'

'No, you need to rest. You don't need me here, I just came to hug you.'

'Oh, please stay!' she protested. 'I feel tired but my mind's whirling and I'm too wired to sleep, so some nice friendly company would be lovely. You can tell me more about Sam.'

'OK, if you're sure?' She perched on the edge of the chair, still holding Annie's hand, and told her about Sam wanting to buy James and Connie's house. 'I've told him he's crazy, because he hasn't even got a proper job—'

'He can have my job,' Annie said instantly.

'He's got your job,' she pointed out, but Annie shook her head.

'No—permanently. I'm not coming back.'

Kate felt her eyes widen. 'Seriously? You're not coming back at all?'

Annie shook her head again.

'I missed so much of the girls when they were tiny because I had to work, and I really, really want to be there for them all this time, so I'm going to stop. I'll be a full-time mum for the first time ever, and I can't wait. Tell James. I'll let him know officially later, but he ought to know, especially as it affects you and Sam.'

Kate nodded. It could mean that they'd stay in Yoxburgh near their friends—living in James and Connie's house? She didn't get that lucky…

'Sure. I'll tell him later, we're seeing them this evening,' she said. 'And I'm really pleased for you, because I know how worried you were about relying on your mother so much, but—oh, I am going to miss working with you.'

'No, you won't! You'll have your own baby,' Annie reminded her gently. 'And you'll be able to come and see me whenever you want.'

'I'll have to go back to work, though,' she said. 'I can't expect Sam to support me. It's only the baby he's interested in.'

Annie eyed her thoughtfully. 'Are you sure about that? Maybe it's the package—the whole deal.'

'What—playing happy families? I don't think so. There's still plenty of chemistry between us, but that's not enough on its own, and I'm not going to get my hopes up. If we can just share the house and the baby without killing each other, I'll be more than happy.'

Annie laughed softly, and rested her head back on the pillow. 'Silly girl. You'll be fine. You'll see...'

Her eyes drifted shut, and after a moment Kate slipped her hand carefully out of Annie's and left her sleeping. She saw Ed on the way out, standing over a crib in SCBU, and he beamed at her and came to the door, his grin nearly splitting his face in two.

'Congratulations, Daddy,' she said with a

smile, and he gave a choked laugh and hugged her hard.

'Thank you. I never thought this would ever happen to me, Kate, and it's just amazing.'

'I'm so pleased for you,' she said, blinking back tears and trying to find a smile. 'So how are they?'

'Incredible. Want to see them?'

She shook her head. 'No. Well, yes, of course I do, I'd love to, but I'd better let Annie show them to me. She's sleeping now, so I left her. Say goodbye to her for me, and well done, both of you.'

She kissed his cheek and left him to his new family, trying really hard not to be jealous of their obvious happiness. And at least Sam was standing by her and the baby and they seemed to be getting on OK. That, frankly, was more than she could have hoped for.

The agent's valuation was neither higher nor lower than Sam had been expecting because he'd had no idea what the house would be worth, but it fell within his budget which was all that mattered, and he told James so.

'So, can I bring Kate round this evening to look at it?' he asked again, and James shrugged.

'Sure. The others are coming at seven thirty. Do you want to come before or after?'

'Before. I don't want you getting all random on me and accepting their offer before you have a chance to hear mine.'

James laughed. 'As if. Come round as soon as you finish. Connie'll be busy with Joseph, but I'm sure she won't mind if you just wander round and make yourselves at home.'

He sent Kate a text, and she rang him straight back.

'Fabulous,' she said, sounding unusually cheerful. 'Pick me up from mine as soon as you're done.'

'Ten minutes?'

'Perfect. I've got some news for you, too. Bye.'

'News?'

The phone went dead, and he slid it back into his pocket and frowned.

News? News about what? Unless…

He finished off the paperwork on his last patient, handed over to the registrar and headed straight for her flat.

* * *

She was sitting outside on the low garden wall, and she jumped up the moment she saw him approach and got straight into the car.

'Annie's leaving,' she said without preamble. 'She's got to tell James officially, but she's not coming back to work ever.'

'Wow. Is it still under wraps?'

She shook her head, but then pulled a face. 'Well, sort of. She wants me to tell James, but until she's done it officially I suppose it shouldn't be broadcast. So it looks as though you might have a job.'

'If James can rig the interview panel,' he said, showing the first slight glimmer of doubt she'd seen from him, but she just laughed.

'You'll get it. Our ED has been notoriously difficult to find staff for, maybe because James has such high standards, maybe because they just don't want to work in what they perceive as a provincial centre, but trust me, if James thinks you're qualified, you're in. Well, barring flood, fire, civil commotion and acts of God— isn't that what they say in insurance documents as the get-out clause?'

He laughed. 'Something like that,' he said, and then he leant across and kissed her, taking her breath away.

'So, what do you think of it? Is it big enough? Could you live here?'

They'd worked their way up through the house and were standing in James and Connie's bedroom on the top floor, looking out of the huge east-facing roof lights, and all she could see was the sea and sky.

'Big enough? Are you crazy? It's got four bedrooms, a fabulous living space, stunning sea views, a garden—it's even got an en suite! I've never had any of those things in my life, Sam! Could I live here? Absolutely. Can you afford it?'

'Yes.'

Just that, no hesitation.

She turned and stared out of the window again, watching the light playing on the surface of the waves, listening to the sound of the sea breaking on the shingle, and she wanted to cry.

Instead she closed her eyes, counted to ten and turned back to him.

'Then buy it, if you want it, if you think it's

the right thing to do. It's not really up to me, it's your money, and you'll have to firm the job up with James, but I can't tell you what to do.'

'But—in principle? Does it tick all the boxes on your wish list?'

She just laughed. 'Sam, my wish list is a roof over my head, security, central heating and preferably no noisy neighbours partying all night. Trust me, I'm not hard to please.'

He drew in a long, slow breath and let it out again, then gave her a wry smile. 'Kerry had a wish list as long as your arm. She knew exactly what she wanted, how she wanted it, what colours, what materials—'

'I'm not Kerry,' she said softly, and he frowned slightly.

'No. No, you're not, are you?' he said thoughtfully, as if he'd just discovered something new and rather interesting, and then he nodded and gestured towards the stairs.

'Better go and tell them, then, hadn't we?' he said, and she wasn't sure but she had a feeling she might just have earned some brownie points…

* * *

'We want it.'

James nodded slowly. 'OK, but timing's crucial, Sam, and I can't get you a definite job offer yet. Annie has to make it official, and then we have to go through all the hoops—not that that'll be a problem unless you blot your copybook between now and then.'

'I have no plans to do that,' he said with a smile, 'and if the job doesn't materialise, it'll be a sound investment anyway. And the tenants definitely want my house. They'll move fast.'

James nodded again. 'OK. What about the price?'

'I'm not going to make you a cheeky offer, if that's what you mean,' he said with a laugh. 'We'll give you the asking price, and if it should go to a bidding war—'

'It won't. If you're sure you can deliver and it means we get our new house, then it's yours.'

His.

'Wow,' he said softly. Little more than a week ago, he'd had nothing to look forward to. Now, suddenly, everything was falling into place in the most unlikely way, and it felt like the sun had come out from behind the blackest cloud.

He was speechless for a second, then he felt his face crack into a smile he had no hope of suppressing. 'That's amazing,' he said, and shook hands with James, then hugged him just for good measure. 'Thank you.'

'Don't thank me. I want your money,' James said with a grin, and Sam laughed and turned to Kate.

'Woo-hoo! We're going to have a house!' he said, the smile still plastered all over his face, and he picked her up in his arms and hugged her.

'Put me down,' she said with a breathless laugh, and he lowered her slowly to the floor, her body in contact with his from head to toe, and then just because he couldn't help himself any longer, he bent his head, cupped her face in his hands and kissed her.

'Are we celebrating something?' Connie asked, coming into the room behind him, and he let go of Kate and hugged Connie, too.

'Absolutely. You're talking to the next owners of your house.'

'Really? Are you sure? It's not just because

of the boat, is it? Because we can work round that, Sam. Or because we need a quick sale? For God's sake don't be noble.'

He stared at her in disbelief, and then laughed, the joy bubbling up in him like fine champagne.

'No, Connie. There's no way I'm that noble. Not by a country mile. I want this house—*we* want this house—not because the boat's a pain or you want to move, but because we love it, pure and simple, don't we?'

He looked at Kate, and she smiled at him. 'Yes, we do,' she said softly, and Connie grinned.

'Right, well, in that case, James, get on the phone and cancel the viewing tonight, and then crack open the Prosecco. I think it's time we had a party!'

CHAPTER EIGHT

SHE HARDLY DRANK any Prosecco, and nor did Connie, but it didn't stop them celebrating.

Not that the celebration was really about her, she knew that, but the spin-off was that she might, if it all worked out, end up living in the sort of house that she'd never even dared to fantasise about.

But only if she and Sam could live together, and the worry about that was still niggling at her. Only one way to find out, though, and that was to get on with it, so when James offered Sam another glass and he hesitated, she chipped in.

'I could always drive, if I'm insured?'

Sam frowned thoughtfully at her. 'Yes, it's insured for anyone over twenty-five with a clean licence, but that won't help me get back here tonight, though.'

'So stay at mine,' she said, and met his searching eyes.

He held hers for a breathless moment, then turned to James and held his glass out.

'In that case—'

She felt her heart thud as he turned back, met her eyes again and raised the filled glass a fraction, in a silent toast.

Or a promise?

She unlocked the door at the top of the stairs, pushed it open and walked into the kitchen on legs that weren't quite steady.

'Do you want coffee?' she asked over her shoulder, only to find he was right behind her.

'Not really. Shall I make up the spare bed?'

'Only if you want to,' she replied, her heart in her mouth, and held her breath for his answer.

She felt the soft brush of air against her cheek, the touch of his hand on her shoulder turning her slowly towards him, saw the pulse beating at the base of his throat before he tilted her head up to meet his eyes.

How could ice smoulder?

'You know what I want,' he said quietly, his eyes locked on hers, searching for her answer, 'but I need you to be sure.'

She swallowed, hesitating for a fraction of a second before she lifted her hand up and laid it against his jaw, feeling the slight graze of stubble against her palm, the heat of his breath as she trailed her thumb over his lips.

His eyes held hers, the fire in them burning all the way down through her body and setting it alight with need.

'I'm sure,' she murmured, moving her hand and drawing his head down to meet her lips, and his breath hitched as his eyes closed and he eased her hard up against him, one hand cradling her head, the other cupping her bottom and lifting her closer as the fire in her raged out of control.

She pressed her hands against his chest and pushed him gently away. 'Not here,' she said breathlessly. 'My room.'

How could it be so good?

He shifted to his side and trailed his free hand slowly down over her throat, across her shoulder, down her arm, across her hip, coming to rest over the gentle curve where his child lay sheltered.

'Hello, baby,' he murmured, stroking his hand lightly over it, and then he shifted his attention higher, back to Kate, studying her intently. 'Your body's changing,' he said softly, his hand moving on, gliding back up to cradle the soft fullness of the breast nearest to him, the nipple darkened from rose to dusk by her hormones. He brushed his thumb over it and it peaked obligingly, making him smile.

'Why did you tell me you were a glamour model?' he asked idly, his thumb still toying with her nipple.

She gave a tiny shrug. 'I don't know. I was sick of men either fantasising about me in uniform or telling me their health issues, I suppose. And it wasn't an outright lie. I have done it.'

His hand stilled. 'Really? When? Why?'

'For money. I was eighteen, I was about to start my nursing course and I was broke. I didn't want a massive student loan and a friend was doing it, and she persuaded me to go with her.'

'And?' he asked, sensing that there was more, and she sighed.

'And it paid well, but I hated it. I hated having to put my body on show, but I needed the money. And then this guy—well, let's just say he wanted what he thought was on offer. So I stopped doing it and focused on my studies.'

He sensed a world of unspoken words, and his gut tightened. 'Did he hurt you?'

She shook her head. 'No. Not my body.'

'Just your spirit.'

'My pride? My dignity? My sense of self-worth? Not that it wasn't already in the gutter.' She closed her eyes, and he leant in and kissed her gently.

'I'm sorry.'

They opened again. 'Don't be. It was a steep but valuable learning curve.'

'Sounds like the rest of your life.' He cupped her cheek, turning her head towards him and kissing her again before rolling onto his back and drawing her gently into his arms.

'Tell me about it,' he murmured as she settled against him. 'Your life. What happened, where you lived, who opened your post—who made you think you ruin everybody's lives.'

She gave a short, sad huff of laughter. 'Have you got all night?'

'If that's what it takes.'

So she told him, hesitantly at first, then as he felt the tension go out of her, more fluidly, moving through her mother's desertion to the foster parents who fought about her and drove her out.

'I heard them fighting, him yelling, "That bloody girl's ruined everything!", and so I ran away.'

'How old were you then?' he asked, appalled.

'Eight? I'd been there over two years, and all I can remember is them fighting the whole time, and then he said all that and left, slamming the door so hard I thought it was going to break, so I got my things and I ran away.'

'So what happened then?'

'Another failed foster placement, and then social services put me into a home because it was my fault, apparently, because I was disruptive, so I was there until I was nearly eleven and hated every minute of it. And then they found me some new foster parents, a professional couple with a younger child, which was so much better. She'd been a nurse, he was a teacher, and they were wonderful people, but after a while their son started to resent me, and when the son hit puberty...'

She broke off, pressing her lips together, and he hugged her gently, unsure of what was coming, sure he wouldn't like it.

'Go on.'

'He didn't respect my boundaries. He used to walk into my bedroom when I was dressing and sit on the bed and watch me and refuse to get out. One day I caught him in my underwear drawer. Another day I found him reading my diary—'

'Which is why you didn't want me to open your post for you?'

She nodded. 'I told him to leave me alone, to keep out of my room, but he wouldn't, and every time they heard us shouting he blamed me, so I told them what he was doing and they gave him hell and grounded him, but that just made him worse.'

'How?'

'Oh, you know kids. There's no end to the subtle cruelties they can inflict when there's nobody looking, but that wasn't enough for him. He wanted more, and he wanted me out, so he waited until we were alone in the house one day, and then he tried to rape me.'

Sam swore, softly and viciously, and his arms tightened reflexively around her. 'What did you do? Did you report him?'

'What was the point? He would just have lied, like he always lied, so I did the only thing I could do. I ran away, which was exactly what he wanted.'

'Where did you go?'

'The park. I hid from the park keepers, but there were some really dodgy people there, a lot of drugs, deals going down, and I didn't feel safe. His parents had given me a mobile and I didn't answer it, but in the end I was so scared I rang them and they got the police to open the gates and let me out.'

'Jeez, Kate. What did the police do?'

'Nothing. I told them I'd got shut in there by accident and they believed me, but my foster parents didn't, and they were worried sick.'

'I'll bet they were. And the boy?' he asked. 'What happened to him?'

He felt her shrug. 'He wouldn't tell them what had happened and nor would I, I just said I couldn't stay there anymore, so social services found me a place to live while I finished my

A-levels, and they kept an eye on me. My foster father gave me private tuition because he knew how important my future was to me, and my foster mother helped me with my entry for nursing, so without them I wouldn't be where I am today, but I didn't feel truly free of him until I was at uni.'

She ground to a halt, and he rested his head against hers and sighed quietly. 'Oh, Kate. I'm so sorry. No wonder you've got issues. And I thought my life was tough because I got sent to boarding school.'

'I don't suppose it was so very different to being in care.'

He gave a hollow laugh. 'I don't know. Probably not, really, except I imagine you were mostly with underprivileged kids who had an excuse, and I was with spoilt little rich kids who just expected Mummy and Daddy to buy them out of trouble and didn't give a damn who they hurt. I expect the end result was much the same.'

'Kids are kids, Sam. They can be amazing, and they can be unspeakably cruel. But you learn how to keep out of the way, and you move on and try not to make the same mistakes over and over again, but it doesn't always work and you never really forget. It's always there, lurking in the background, waiting for an unguarded moment, which is why I don't talk about it.'

Her hand came up and cupped his cheek, her face tilting up to his as she turned his head so she could kiss him. 'Make love to me, Sam,' she whispered. 'Make me forget it all.'

How could he refuse? That first night, he'd used her to help him forget his grief, so he knew that it worked, if only for a while. He could do the same for her.

He threaded his fingers through her hair, cradled her head and kissed her back until there was nothing left in the world but him and her, and the fire raging between them burned away the pain.

They were nearly late for work, not least because they'd woken late and shared the shower to save time, which had nearly derailed them completely.

'Later,' he promised, towelling himself roughly dry as he left the bathroom, and she bit her lip to stop the smile, dragged the knots out of her hair, cleaned her teeth and ran to the bedroom, to find him dressed in the clean clothes he'd grabbed from the cabin the night before on their way home.

He was the only tidy thing in the bedroom, and she scooped up a pile of washing, threw it out of the way, found some clean underwear and clothes and followed him downstairs to the car with ten minutes to go before their shifts started.

'Cutting it fine,' James said drily as they walked in, and she saw Sam's lips twitch, which just gave her the giggles.

'Hussy,' he muttered. 'You'll give us away.'

'And the whisker-burn won't? And anyway, do you really think there's anyone in the hospital now who doesn't know we're an item? Dream on.'

'Well, we'd better give them something to talk about, then,' he said, setting the smile free, and pulling her to a halt he dropped a kiss on her startled lips and walked away, whistling softly to himself.

'Whoa. He is smokin' hot!' Petra said, coming up behind her and gazing after Sam.

'Petra! I haven't seen you for ages. How was your holiday? Did you have a good time?'

'Not as good as you, apparently,' Petra said, her eyes still on Sam. 'We need to go out tonight, and you can tell me all.'

She gave a slightly crazed laugh, and shook her head. 'I can't go out tonight, I'm busy, and anyway, I wouldn't know where to start. Well, I would. January.'

'He's the hot guy?' Petra squealed, and Kate flipped her mouth shut with a finger and wondered why she'd told her friend so much.

'Shh. Actually, it's all a bit more than that. We're—' She didn't know quite where to take that one, so backtracked hastily. 'Look, I'll tell you another time, but there is one thing. We're having a baby.'

Petra's mouth fell open again. 'Oh, my… Kate, are you OK? What are you going to do? Are you getting rid of it?'

'No! And keep your voice down,' she hissed. 'Nobody knows, and it hasn't been easy. His fiancée died two years ago.'

Petra's eyes widened, and she grabbed Kate's hand. 'Honey, are you OK? Seriously? Because that sounds like a whole cartload of baggage. If I was you I'd run for the hills.'

Yes, you would, she thought, and a few days ago she would have done, too, but now nothing was further from her mind and she wondered what on earth she and Petra had really had in common, apart from both being single.

'I'm fine,' she said, then glanced at the clock and yelped. 'Seriously, I have to get to work. I'm not even in scrubs and I'm ten minutes late. I'll see you later.'

'Promise?'

'I promise. I'll call you, if nothing else.'

She fled, changed at the speed of light and reached the doors of Resus at the same time as the patient who was being wheeled in.

Sam was there waiting, and he frowned questioningly and mouthed, 'Are you all right?'

She was, she realised. Very all right. She smiled back, nodded and took her place in the team.

Annie sent her a text during the morning, and she skipped her lunch break with Sam and ran up to Maternity and found her in SCBU with a baby in her arms.

She beckoned her in, and Kate gowned up and went over to her, giving her a careful hug.

'Hi, I got your text. So who's this? He's gorgeous.'

'Theo. Here, sit down and give him a cuddle.'

'Are you sure? He's so tiny—I don't think I've ever held a baby this small before.'

'Ah, well, you'd better start practising. Here you go.'

And there she was, with another baby in her arms, but so tiny this time, so precious, so fragile, and she felt a surge of protectiveness and fear in equal measure.

'Oh, Annie,' she breathed, staring at him as if he was the most amazing thing she'd ever seen, and right then he opened his eyes and stared up at her, and she blinked.

'Oh, he's so like Ed!'

'I know. It's hilarious. He's so tiny, but he's Ed to a T.'

'And the other one?'

'He's like me. We've called him Freddie, for my father,' she said, a tender, bittersweet smile on her face. 'He would have loved them all so much...'

'Oh, Annie,' she said again, and then laughed at herself. 'I'm sounding like a stuck record,' she said a little unevenly, and looked down at Theo again, at the tiny face the image of his father's, and she wondered if her baby would be like Sam. She hoped so. 'I can't believe this is going to happen to me,' she said softly, and Annie reached out a hand and squeezed her shoulder.

'Get used to it. It's amazing.'

'It's terrifying.'

'Well, that, too, but you soon get used to it.' She searched Kate's eyes. 'So how are things with Sam? Did you like the house?'

'I loved the house,' she said. 'There was nothing not to love about it. And—Sam stayed with me last night. He's moving in later, properly.'

'Oh, Kate, that's wonderful!'

'Well, I hope so. It is at the moment, I just hope it lasts. Wish us luck.'

'You don't need luck, you need guts and determination and compassion, and you've got all that in spades. You'll be fine, Kate. You wait and see.'

Theo started to cry then, so Annie held her arms out and winced, and Kate felt a pang of guilt as she handed the baby over.

'I haven't even asked how you are,' she said lamely, and Annie gave a wry laugh.

'Oh, I'm a bit sore, but so, so happy.'

'Worth it, then?'

'Oh, yes.' She gave a contented, happy laugh and looked back down at the baby in her arms, her face softened by love. 'Every single moment.'

Sam moved in properly that night, and while he packed up the cabin and discussed solicitors and timescales with James and Connie, she loaded the washing machine, blitzed the bedroom and scrubbed the bathroom within an inch of its life.

By the time he got back with all his things, the bed was made up with fresh linen, and she'd cleared space for him in the wardrobe in the spare bedroom, consigning the other half to charity shop bags.

And her spare set of keys were on his pillow in her room.

He picked them up, hefted them in his hand and smiled. 'Thank you.'

'Don't thank me. It's only so I don't have to run downstairs and let you in all the time,' she teased, and he chucked them back on the bed, pulled her into his arms and kissed her, then looked around and blinked.

'Good grief, you've been busy.'

'I needed to be, it was a slum.'

'Not quite.'

'Verging on it. I've made you space in the wardrobe next door for shirts and stuff, and there's a drawer in there for your underwear.'

He nodded. 'Thanks. Have you eaten?'

She shook her head. 'No, not really. I was waiting for you, but I've grazed on a ton of chocolate. You?'

'Connie fed me a sandwich, but that's all and it was ages ago. Want me to cook while you put your feet up?'

'No. I've got some stuff in the freezer. Why don't I do it while you unpack?' she said, touched that he'd offered, and she was almost done when he came up behind her, put his arms around her and rested his chin on her shoulder.

'So what are we having?' he asked, nuzzling her ear.

She laughed. 'Well, I thought it was chilli, so I cooked some rice, but turns out it's Bolognese sauce.'

She felt his chuckle through her shoulders. 'I'm sure it won't kill us,' he said, and for a second the words echoed in the air around them before he straightened up and moved away, his warmth replaced by a chilling draught that came from nowhere.

'I'll get the plates,' he said, and she stood at the sink draining and rinsing the rice and wondering if Kerry's ghost would overshadow them for ever.

They ate their meal in a polite silence, hardly exchanging a word, and when it was finished he thanked her, cleared the table and ran the water to wash up.

'I can do that—'

'No. Go and put your feet up. You've done enough today.'

He should have turned and smiled at her, soft-ened it, but he couldn't meet her wounded gaze, and as he heard her leave the room, he plunged his hands into the hot water, leant over the sink and closed his eyes.

Just when it was all going so well, he thought, and swallowed a block of emotion that threat-ened to choke him. The grief he recognised, but guilt, too—guilt for betraying Kerry by moving on so readily with Kate, guilt for short-chang-ing Kate because a part of his heart would al-ways be with Kerry, guilt for fathering a child in such unpromising circumstances—the list of his emotional crimes was endless, and he had an overwhelming urge to curl up in the corner and cry, but he'd done enough of that.

More than enough. It was time to man up and deal with reality.

He finished the washing up, wiped down the kitchen, cleared and polished the sink—Kerry there again, being fastidious beyond reason—and stuck his head round the door.

'Can I get you a drink?'

She shook her head. She'd turned away from

him so he couldn't see her face, but he knew with a sickening certainty that she'd been crying.

He went over to her, crouched down in front of her and turned her face towards him, tsking softly at the clumped lashes and the dribble of mascara sliding down her cheek.

'I'm sorry,' he said heavily.

'Don't be. It's too soon for you, I know that.'

Her voice was cracking, and he shifted to the seat beside her and drew her into his arms with a sigh.

'It's two years, Kate, I should be over it, but sometimes it just creeps up on me and takes me by surprise. One of those unguarded moments you were talking about last night, I guess, but it's not a part of us, of what we have.'

'Yes, it is, because I'm just a constant reminder of what you've lost. I'm just there, in your face, getting in the way of your memories, being the wrong person in the wrong place at the wrong time, and I can't do it, Sam. I can't compete with her for your affection—'

'You don't have to! This is nothing to do with her, and you're not the wrong person, Kate, you're just you.'

'And that's supposed to be a good thing?'

He let out a sigh. 'Yes. Yes, it is, for us. I wasn't trying to replace her—I wasn't trying to do anything when I met you except forget, just for a little while. I certainly didn't expect this to happen, but it has, and, no, it's not the same, but that doesn't make it bad or unworkable. It just takes getting used to, and that's going to take time, but we'll get there.'

She nodded, snuggling closer, sniffing a little until he handed her a tissue.

'Here. Blow your nose. I'll get you tea.'

He brought it in, but she didn't linger after she'd finished it, just took her mug back to the kitchen when the programme she was watching ended, and told him she was going to turn in.

'Don't feel you have to rush, I just fancy an early night,' she said, and went into the bedroom and pushed the door to.

He stared at it for an age, then dropped his head back and let out a long, quiet sigh. She hadn't shut it completely. He supposed that was a signal that he was still welcome in her bed, but maybe just not yet.

He'd give it a while, he decided, and then go

and join her, but he wouldn't expect a rapturous welcome—unlike last night, when she'd opened her heart to him and told him the story of her sad and fractured childhood. Well, the walls were up again now, without a doubt, and he had to respect her boundaries.

He turned off the television, washed up their mugs and went quietly into the bedroom, undressing and slipping into bed beside her without disturbing her.

'Night, Kate,' he murmured, but there was silence, so he punched the pillow, turned away from her and closed his eyes.

No good. She wasn't asleep. He could tell because her breathing was too even, too measured, too—conscious?

He rolled onto his back and turned his head towards her. 'Kate?'

In the dim light from the streetlamp outside he saw the soft sheen of tears on her cheek, and with another wave of guilt and regret he rolled towards her, pulled her into his arms and kissed her tears away.

'Don't shut me out, Kate,' he murmured. 'I'm sorry I hurt you—'

'You didn't hurt me. I just can't be her—'

'You don't have to be her. Just be you. There's nothing wrong with you.' He kissed her again, trailing his lips over her cheek, her nose, her eyes, then down again to her mouth, taking it in a long, slow, tender kiss that made her sigh.

He felt the tension go out of her, her arms creep round him, and he gave a quiet sigh of relief, shifted her further into his arms and held her as she settled into sleep.

CHAPTER NINE

IT WAS DIFFERENT after that.

They'd stopped being so wary around each other, having to weigh every word, and they settled into a comfortable routine. She'd thought it would be difficult, that she'd find it hard to have him there all the time, day and night, but it grew easier with every passing day.

They told some of the people at work, of course, and got mixed reactions, but she'd expected that and she knew some of them would be waiting for her to mess up, but she was determined not to, and she kept her head down and avoided the doom-mongers, and gradually it slid down the gossip charts.

They'd been sharing the flat over a week when they heard that Tom, the young man who'd had the cardiac arrest, was out of danger, and Sam went up to see him and brought her back a celebratory coffee from the canteen.

'How is he?' she asked, conscious of the fact that Sam had found his case especially hard, but he was genuinely happy.

'He's great. He's got a long way to go, but he'll get there. I'm just so relieved for him. Oh, by the way, the house paperwork came through in the post this morning after you left. We need to sign the contract and get it back.'

'Wow. That was quick!'

'It had to be. Right, I'd better get on.'

He dropped a kiss on her lips, lingered just a moment too long and then winked as he walked away, and her heart gave a happy little jiggle.

They exchanged contracts on the house within the four weeks James had stipulated, and then he started to make lists of things they'd need.

Lists of furniture, lists of curtains, lists for the kitchen, for the nursery—it was only the nursery that really interested her, and for the first time she expressed a preference.

'I want white. White everything. It's easier.'

'I thought babies were supposed to have bright, stimulating colours?'

'Not in their bedrooms,' she said, although

she didn't actually know that for a fact, but she knew if she was in a room filled with colour it was harder to settle to sleep, whereas a white room with soft grey and putty accents lowered her stress levels and soothed her instantly. 'And anyway,' she added, 'I don't want to get anything yet. Not so soon.'

'We can still look. Let's go shopping,' he said, turning off his tablet with its endless images and pulling her to her feet.

'What—now?' she said, hanging back, because she still didn't really feel it was her house, and she didn't want to make a massive emotional investment in it. In her mind it was something he and Kerry had done, and she just felt it would be an utter minefield.

'Yes, now. It's Saturday morning, the shops are open, we can go and wander round them and choose what you like.'

'Sam, I really don't mind—'

'Of course you do. I know you're being noble because you think it's my house, but it's not, it's our house, and I want you to like it and help me make it a home, so stop being so noncommittal and tell me what you like or we won't have a stick of furniture to sit on.'

Was she being noble or noncommittal? Or was it that she wanted so badly for it to feel like home that it was terrifying her?

'Sam, I'm not like Kerry, these things really don't matter to me,' she said, and he frowned and let go of her hand and sat down again.

'I know you're not like her. I'm well aware of that. If I was with Kerry doing this, I'd be trailing round behind her ticking her lists and agreeing just for the sake of peace. I don't think it even occurred to her to ask me what I wanted. She was just like a kid in a sweetshop.'

She stared at him in astonishment. 'Gosh,' she said softly, after an age. 'Where did that come from?'

He shrugged. 'It's the truth. It didn't stop me loving her, it's just how she was. She was sweet, kind, funny, generous, but she didn't have a spontaneous bone in her body. She was meticulously organised, fanatically tidy, she planned everything down to the last detail—nothing was allowed to happen by chance. And I still feel guilty that I didn't take any interest, that

I was glad I was out of the country when she was planning the wedding, because she would have driven me mad with the endless trivia. But you're not her, and nor am I, and I really have no idea where to start, so your help would be very much appreciated.'

He fell silent, and she let out a long, soft sigh and wrapped her arms around him. 'Oh, Sam. I'm sorry. I didn't know that. Of course I'll come shopping with you.'

It turned out that she did have opinions, and it surprised her.

'How about this?' Sam would ask, and she'd frown and he'd laugh and walk on. 'This?' Frown, laugh, walk on.

They left that shop, because in fact neither of them liked anything they had in stock, and went to the next one and tried again.

'Oh, this is better,' she said instantly as they walked in, and he smiled.

'I'm glad we agree. So—sofas?'

'I like this one.' She sat down, leant back and shook her head and got up. 'You can't slouch in it.'

'Well, that's a must. Let's find a slouchy one,' he said, and threading his fingers through hers he led her round the displays until they found one with the right degree of slouchiness.

He sat down at one end, and she sat at the other, swivelled her legs round and put her feet in his lap.

'Perfect,' she said with a grin, and he chuckled.

'I agree. I think we should have a pair, like James and Connie. What about the fabric?'

'I like this leather,' she said. 'It's nice—sort of battered and not intimidating. And you can wipe leather. Babies are very messy, from my limited experience. They tend to leak a bit.'

He stifled a laugh and hailed an assistant who'd been hovering discreetly in the background.

'How long will they take to come?' Sam asked. 'Because we need this quickly. We're moving in a couple of weeks.'

'Well, you're in luck, then, if you like this, because our sale starts tomorrow, and all our display stock is going to be marked down. Otherwise it'll be six weeks.'

'So we could have this one sooner?'

'Yes. And if you wanted a pair, we have another one in the window.'

'Perfect,' Sam said. 'Do you do beds?'

Of course they did, and to Kate's relief they'd all be discounted, too. They'd almost agreed on a painted wooden bed when they went round the corner and he spotted a different one.

'How about this for the master bedroom?' he said, pointing at a huge mahogany sleigh bed, and she nodded slowly.

'That's lovely. It looks welcoming.'

'After a long, hard shift, bed is *always* welcoming,' he said drily, and lay down on it. 'Oh, yes. Try the mattress,' he coaxed, patting the other side, and she lay down, feeling like an idiot, and then totally forgot to care how she looked, because it was bliss.

'That's amazing,' she said softly. 'It's like lying on a cloud. How much is it?'

He laughed and told her you couldn't put a price on a comfortable bed, which by extension meant it was shockingly expensive, and then reminded her it would be in the sale.

'Well, it's your money,' she said, getting up reluctantly. 'Don't forget we'll need something for the spare bedroom, as well, before you blow the entire budget on this one.'

'Don't worry about the budget. Now, is it big enough, or do we need a super-king? By the time the kids are in it, too...'

Kids? *Kids?* She was still getting her head around the one they were having, and he was planning *more*?

'I think you're getting ahead of yourself,' she said quietly, and the smile on his face disappeared in an instant.

'Yeah. Sorry. Anyway, the super-king might not go up the stairs.'

He cleared his throat and moved away from her, from the blissful but contentious bed, from the idea of a huge, happy family bouncing around in it, and after confirming the details with the assistant, he shot her a glance.

'Coffee?'

She nodded, ready to sit down on something she didn't have to have an opinion on, and they went into the store's café. He sent her to find a seat, and came over with coffees and a huge slab of chocolate fudge cake.

'What's that?'

'A peace offering.'

She looked up at him, at his sombre eyes, his mouth set in a tight line of regret, and she shook her head.

'Oh, Sam. It's OK. It's just that I'm still coming to terms with having *this* baby, and with the idea of living with you, and frankly that's hard enough to get my head round.'

'Yeah. Baby steps. I'm sorry.' He sat down, handed her one of the two forks and smiled wryly. 'Can we share?'

She smiled back at him. 'Since you ask so nicely.'

'Hmph.' He scooped off a chunk and inhaled it, and she laughed.

'Shopping getting to you?'

'Absolutely,' he groaned. 'I don't know how women have the stamina for it.'

'Me, neither. Maybe it helps if it's someone else's money, but I've never been in that position so I wouldn't know.'

'You are now.'

She shook her head. 'No. This stuff is for your house—'

'Our house. I'm putting it in joint names.'

She felt the blood drain from her face, then surge back up. 'Sam—no! Why? That's not fair! It's your money, from the house you bought with Kerry. You can't give it away!'

He stared at her, obviously shocked. 'It's not like it was ever our home, Kate. I told you that.'

'But it should have been your home,' she said, her eyes filling for a woman who never got to live in it, never got to realise her dream, and Sam gave a soft groan and covered her hand with his.

'Kate—let's not do this here.'

'Why not? We're getting in so deep, Sam, and you're just being noble and doing the decent thing and you're not ready—'

'It's not about being ready, Kate, it's about reality, and what's happening to us, whether we're ready or not. The baby won't wait, and it needs a home.'

'Then put it in the baby's name,' she said desperately.

He sighed and shook his head slowly. 'Do you really hate Kerry that much?'

'What? No, of course I don't, but it was her dream home—'

'Not mine, though. It was sensible, manageable

for her on her own while I was away, and close to her parents so that if anything happened to me she'd have their support. It was me who was supposed to die, not her, which was why I just let her do what she wanted with it, but I could never have been truly happy there. It was too far from the sea, too hemmed in by other houses, too—hell, I don't know, too suburban. I don't think we would have stayed there that long. It just wasn't me.'

'And this one is,' she said slowly, knowing it was true.

'It is. It's so perfect for me I can't believe I'm going to live in it. I've always loved it, since the first moment I saw it, and if it makes you feel any better, no, Kerry never saw it.'

He fell silent while she assimilated all of that, and the thing that came to the top of the pile was his bald statement that he was the one who was supposed to die.

'You've got survivor guilt,' she said softly, and he nodded.

'Yes. Yes, I suppose I have, in a way. She was in a safe place, while I was out in the field with bombs going off all around me, snipers trying to pick me off when we flew in to rescue some-one who'd been ambushed by an IED—it was a miracle I didn't get hurt, but I got away without a scratch, and she…'

He broke off, stirred his coffee absently and then looked up and met her eyes.

'Look, I know it's tough for you, but I don't want it to be. None of that is anything to do with you, it's all in the past. We're buying the house now, it needs furniture, it's going to be our home. It's a new start, Kate. A new start I desperately need. Please, don't make it harder for either of us than it already is.'

She felt her eyes welling, blinked away the tears and nodded. 'Of course. I'm sorry. Let's just have our coffee and get on with it, shall we? We've still got a lot to do.'

Kate crawled up the stairs, plopped onto the sofa and put her feet up.

'I'm never going shopping again,' she groaned, and Sam laughed, bent over the back of the sofa and dropped a kiss on her head.

'Well, at least it's done now, or most of it. I

can't believe the trivia, though—so many decisions about nothing that matters.'

She turned her head round and peered at him over the back of the sofa as he went into the kitchen. 'So you agree with me, then, that it doesn't matter?'

He laughed. 'I didn't say that. It's just that when you have to make decisions about what kind of cutlery, which glasses, crockery, tea towels, for heaven's sake—it's just endless!'

She followed him into the kitchen, trying not to laugh. 'So were you just passing the buck, then, making me choose so you didn't have to commit?'

'Damn. You rumbled me.'

He chuckled and pulled her in for a hug, and she rested her head on his chest and sighed. 'Oh, Sam. Are we really going to be OK?'

'Yes. Now go and sit down, and I'll make you tea and try and work out what we've got to eat. Or we could order a takeaway?'

'What, make another decision?' she said, and they both started to laugh, clinging to each other and laughing until their sides ached, and then he stared down at her, still in his arms, and bent his head and kissed her.

It wasn't passionate, it didn't linger, it was just—'healing' was the only word she could come up with, building a bridge over the rivers of grief and doubt and insecurity that ran between them, and she realised she felt safe.

Safe with Sam, with life, but also with her future, because for the first time ever, she had one that she might just be able to rely on.

The days ticked by, and before they knew it the twenty-week anomaly scan for the baby was coming up, and so was the move.

They had less than two weeks before the sale was due to be completed, so the furniture delivery was due for the Friday after that, giving them the weekend to unpack everything and settle in before they were back at work on the Monday.

And in the meantime, he thought, watching Kate across the ED, he needed to make a new will and get Kate named as the beneficiary on his forces and NHS pensions. Just in case, because, as he knew only too well, life didn't come with any guarantees.

He added that to his ever-growing 'to-do' list, and gave a wry smile. Kerry would have laughed her socks off at the very thought, but then her 'to-do' list used to start with 'Wake up'. He wondered what she would have made of the spontaneous loose cannon that was Kate, and decided she would have liked her, even though she probably wouldn't have understood her at all.

He was beginning to, and he was discovering a thoughtful, sensitive, compassionate woman with a huge heart and enormous courage. Not to mention a wicked sense of humour and the ability to charm the devil incarnate into submitting to a procedure that was definitely not on his wish list. And on that subject…

He capped his pen, tucked the list into the pocket of his scrubs and went to help her talk Mr Lucas round.

'He's a nightmare,' she said with a sigh after Mr Lucas had finally allowed them to dress his ulcer. 'He's probably the worst of our frequent flyers. He never takes care of himself, he treats us like his personal doctors' surgery and complains bitterly about everything we do for him. I swear, I could kill him sometimes.'

Sam chuckled and gave her a discreet hug. 'You're wonderful with him. Goodness knows why, he doesn't deserve it.'

'Oh, he's just lonely and his life's a mess. I can understand that, even if it does annoy me. How's your to-do list?'

'Growing,' he said wryly. 'Kerry would have laughed at me.'

She gave a soft chuckle at his expression, the rueful self-mockery echoed in his words, realising with a slight shock that they were talking quite naturally about Kerry, as if she was finally taking her rightful place in the dynamics of their relationship.

'She must have felt about you the way you feel about me, then, because you're way more organised than I'll ever be,' she told him honestly.

'Not at work,' he said, shaking his head. 'At work, you're like a streamlined machine. You don't overlook anything, and even when we're ridiculously busy, you still find time to be kind to the patients and make them feel comfortable and safe. That's a real gift, Kate, and you have it in spades.'

She felt her eyes fill at the sudden unexpected compliment, and blinked and turned away. 'Thank you,' she said softly, and then cleared her throat. 'Right, who's next?'

So this was it.

His own home at last, emptied now of James and Connie's possessions, echoing hollowly as he walked around it, his fingers trailing over the walls, the banisters, the doorframes, coming to rest on the handle of the roof light in the master bedroom.

He tugged it gently and it pivoted open, and he leant out, drew the sea air into his lungs and sighed.

His own home, at last, he thought, and wandered through to the en suite bathroom, throwing open the roof light in there and taking in the spectacular view over the marshes behind the house, lonely, desolate and inhospitable, but teeming with nesting wetland birds at this time of year.

'Hello, house,' he said softly, and turned, looking straight through and out at the sea once more. He could feel it tugging him, the urge to fix up the boat and get out on the sea almost over- whelming, but he had a lot to do before that was even on the bottom of his agenda.

With a sigh he closed the windows and ran back downstairs. He had to get Kate. Her shift should have finished now and she'd want to see it, too, but he'd had a selfish urge to see it alone first. He felt a twinge of guilt for not waiting, but he'd needed it, this quiet time alone with the house to make its acquaintance. Heaven knows the peace won't last long, he thought, with the baby coming in just a few more months.

He paused on the veranda and closed his eyes briefly, sending up a silent prayer to whoever might be listening that it would all work out, that the hell and confusion of the past two years could be laid to rest and he and Kate and the baby could make the family he hadn't even re- alised he needed so much, here in this beautiful and welcoming home.

Then he locked the house, ran down the ve- randa steps and went to fetch Kate.

* * *

'Have you got the keys?'

He nodded and held a bunch out to her. 'That's your set, and we've got two spare sets in case we need them. Are you ready to go?'

'Definitely. Have you been down there yet?'

He hesitated, and she knew instantly that he had, that he didn't want to tell her in case she was somehow disappointed that he hadn't waited for her, but that it had been important for him in some way.

Laying a ghost to rest? She could only hope so.

'Sam, it's fine. I totally get it. Come on, let's go and look together.'

They walked up the veranda steps and he unlocked the door, pushed it open and let her go in first. She stepped over the threshold, crushing a tiny flicker of disappointment that he hadn't carried her over it, but this wasn't a love nest, it was a house that would hopefully turn into a home for their family, and so she walked through the kitchen and into the large open living room with the huge bay window framing the sea.

'OK?'

She turned to him, nodded and slipped her hand into his. 'It's beautiful. I love it.'

'Good. So do I. Let's go and have a look upstairs.'

They wandered round for ages, spotting things they hadn't seen before, like the clever storage in the bathroom, the little train frieze around Joseph's old bedroom, the colourful mural on the wall behind where his cot had been.

'I guess all this will have to go,' he said, and her hands fell automatically to caress her bump.

'Probably. It seems a shame, but if it's a girl she might not be into trains.'

'It might be a boy.'

'Do you mind what it is?'

He shook his head. 'No, not at all. I don't care about anything except that it's healthy.'

'What if there's something wrong with it?' she asked.

'We'll deal with it. It might not be easy, but we'll find a way. What about you? Do you care what it is?'

She shook her head. 'Not really. I think I'd like a girl, just because I know more about them than

I do about boys, but I'm like you, I just want it to be all right.'

He laid his hands over hers, then froze. 'Was that a kick?'

She nodded, pulling her hand out from under his so he could feel it better, and he let out a soft huff of wonder.

'That's amazing. How long have you been able to feel it?'

'A week or so? I wasn't sure at first, but it's been having a good old wriggle today.'

He laughed, then wrapped his arms around her and held her close, and she rested her head on his shoulder and sighed.

'Are you OK?' he murmured.

'Mmm. Just happy.'

'Me, too.' He eased her away, looking down intently into her eyes, and then he slid his hands down her arms and took both her hands in his.

'Marry me, Kate. Please? Let's be a proper family?'

She blinked, then took a tiny step back, mentally as well as physically. 'Why? Why do you want to marry me, Sam? Why can't you just accept what we have?'

'Because I want more? Because I'm old-fashioned and I believe a child's parents should be married?'

She shook her head. 'No. That's not a reason to get married. Plenty of parents aren't—and plenty of those who are get divorced.'

'I know. And I know it's no guarantee of happiness, but you'd be better protected in law if we're married.'

'That's not a good enough reason, Sam. People should only get married because they *love* each other. I'm not going to marry you when I don't think either of us is ready for it. I'll move in with you, I'll live here with you and our baby, but I can't marry you just to make it tidy.'

He dragged his hands down over his face, let out a heavy sigh and shook his head.

'No. I'm sorry. You're right. Maybe I wanted to do it for the wrong reasons, to undo our mistakes.'

'You can't, Sam. Nobody can do that. And right now, neither of us is ready for this step—not yet, at least. And we've got so many other things to think about—moving in here, the scan, getting ready for the baby—it's all too much at once. Give us time—please? Let's see how it goes?'

He nodded, but the happiness she'd seen in his eyes was gone, wiped away by her refusal, and as he turned away she pressed her lips together and blinked away the stinging tears.

CHAPTER TEN

THE FURNITURE CAME on Friday morning, as planned, and immediately it started to look like a home.

He'd taken the day off to supervise, and it had paid off because everything had been put in its intended place, everything unwrapped and the packaging taken away, and he'd even had time to make the beds. All that remained was finding a home for the kitchen things, and that was Kate's province.

She was working, but the moment she finished she drove down and joined him, and her face when she walked in made all the angst and effort worthwhile.

'Oh, Sam—it looks amazing!' She ran her fingers over the back of a sofa and scanned the room. 'I love that table. I'm so glad we chose it and not the other one.'

'I thought you didn't care? I thought it didn't matter?' he teased, and she laughed and hugged him.

'It does matter, of course it matters. If it's not yours, you just accept it, but if it's yours, there's no point in it being wrong for the sake of a bit of effort.'

He chuckled. 'Well, you've changed your tune. Come on, come and see the bedrooms.'

He took her by the hand and led her upstairs, and they paused by the door to the nursery at the foot of the attic stairs.

'It looks so empty,' she said, her hand curving over their baby instinctively as if she feared for it.

Did she? She'd refused to buy anything for it until after the scan, so was she still wondering what would happen if she lost it? God forbid, he thought, but if she did, the nursery would hang over them as a constant reminder of all they'd lost.

'Why don't I redecorate it?' he suggested quickly. 'Paint it white, like you said?'

'Or maybe a pale grey? It faces east, it'll be very light.'

'I'll do it white first. I reckon it'll take a couple

of coats at least to cover the mural. Then you can decide.' He took her shoulders and pointed her towards the attic stairs, patting her on the bottom. 'Come on, come and see our room.'

He followed her up, and she pushed open the door at the top and gasped.

'Oh, Sam, it looks fabulous! I thought the bed would be huge in here, but it's perfect!'

She ran her hand over the bedding—pure white hotel stripe zillion thread count Egyptian cotton, over a goose down duvet, because as he'd said you couldn't put a price on a comfortable bed—and sighed.

'It's gorgeous. The whole house—it's gorgeous. You must be so happy with it.'

Not as happy as he would have been if she'd agreed to marry him, but if she wasn't ready—

'Yes. Yes, I am happy with it,' he said firmly. 'I think it'll suit us very well. Come on, I'm starving, I haven't stopped all day. Let's go to the pub and have dinner, and then go back to yours. We can move in tomorrow.'

In fact it took two days, mostly because he wouldn't let her do any of the carrying, and there was a limit to how much even he could carry down the stairs on his own at once.

Anyway, she had enough to do, because it was ages since all the furniture had been pulled out and the flat needed a serious deep clean, so they emptied her possessions out of one room at a time, and while he ran up and down, she blitzed the nooks and crannies that hadn't seen the light of day for yonks.

'How can you have so many clothes?' he asked on the third pass, and she could see him wondering if there could possibly be enough wardrobe space.

So it was Sunday afternoon by the time everything was moved and her flat was ready to be handed back to the landlord.

'All done?'

She nodded. 'I'll just have one last check. I'll see you downstairs.'

She walked through the rooms alone, saying goodbye to her old life. The end of an era, she thought—and the beginning, hopefully, of a better one? Certainly different.

The rooms were all clean now, but they were tatty, in desperate need of new furnishings, and the contrast between it and Sam's house was shocking.

And yet it had been her sanctuary, a place where she could retreat to lick her wounds, and she was sad and a little afraid to let it go.

She closed the door for the last time, turned and tripped on the torn stair carpet, grabbing the banisters to save herself.

'Kate?'

She heard him run up the stairs three at a time, stopping in front of her, hands on her shoulders.

'Are you all right? What happened?'

'I'm fine. I tripped, that's all.'

He sighed sharply. 'That wretched carpet—it's a miracle you haven't killed yourself on these stairs. Come on, let's go.'

She followed him down, out of the front door, closing it with a solid *thunk* behind her.

Time to move on…

Her twenty-week anomaly scan was on Wednesday evening, three days after they'd moved in, and everything was fine. She hadn't realised how tense she'd been, how worried, and now all she felt was the most enormous sense of relief.

'Do you want to know what it is?' the sonographer asked, and she shrugged.

'Sam?'

'I'm not sure. I'll let you decide.'

'I can't decide!' she wailed, half laughing, and the sonographer smiled.

'I tell you what. Why don't I write it down and put it in an envelope? And then you can think about it.'

'OK,' she said slowly, still massively undecided, so Sam took over.

'Give it to me,' he said with a smile, taking the decision out of her hands and tucking the envelope in his pocket. 'Then she won't be able to open it without convincing me she really wants to.'

They left the hospital and drove home—odd, how she was beginning to call it that in her head, even though she still maintained it was his house.

They picked up fish and chips on the way, and ate them out of the paper, sitting on the veranda watching the sun set over the marshes and listening to the keening of the gulls and the clatter of the rigging on Sam's boat.

'I must get on with it,' he said, staring at it thoughtfully. 'I should be able to get it in the water before the end of the summer. That's what it needs, to be in the water. Wooden boats shrink when you take them out, and then they leak, but it shouldn't by the time I've finished.'

'What about the inside?'

'Oh, it's fine. It needs a good clean and a polish, but the interior was refitted a few years ago and it's more than adequate. I'll take you out in it.'

'While I'm pregnant?' she said, feeling a little frisson of alarm, but he just grinned at her.

'It's got an engine, sweetheart. It's not like a little sailing dinghy, it won't capsize.'

'Good,' she said, and handed him the rest of her chips. 'So, what about this baby? Do we want to know?'

'Do you? Or do you want a surprise? That's what you said before.'

'I know, but…'

'Sleep on it. It doesn't really matter, one way or the other. It is what it is, but at least we know that everything's all right.'

She nodded and thought about it for a moment.

'I feel that, if we know, it might seem more real, as if it's a person and not just a wiggly bump. We could stop call it "it".'

'Up to you,' he said, holding up his hands and passing the buck firmly back to her. 'I can't make that decision for you, Kate. It has to be your choice.'

She took a deep breath. 'Let's open it.'

'Sure? There's no going back.'

'I'm sure.'

He handed her the envelope, and she opened it with trembling fingers and pulled out the slip of paper.

'Turn it over.'

'I can't—'

He held her hand, and together they turned the paper over.

'It's a girl! Oh, Sam, it's a girl, we're going to have a daughter!' she said, and burst into tears.

His arm came round her, holding her against his side, and she swiped away the tears, stroking her bump tenderly.

'I can't believe it's a girl...'

'It's what you wanted.'

'I know. Oh, Sam. She feels so real now.'

He hugged her again, then bent his head and kissed her. 'You'll have to choose a name.'

'No, we will. She's our baby, Sam,' she said, taking his hand and resting it over the baby. 'We'll choose her name together.'

His hand moved, caressing their child, caressing her, and she tilted her head and searched his eyes.

'Do you mind that it's not a boy?'

'No, of course not!' he said softly. 'It really doesn't matter to me so long as you're happy. That's all I want.'

He did. She could see it in his eyes, and it changed everything. She lifted her hand and laid it gently against his cheek.

'Let's get married,' she said impulsively, and his eyes widened.

'I thought you weren't ready?'

'I thought I wasn't, but I think I was just worrying about the scan, and at the time it was all I could think about, that and the move. I was just overwhelmed, but—now, somehow, it seems right.'

'Oh, Kate—'

He lowered his head and kissed her tenderly, and she could feel he was shaking. 'Are you sure?' he murmured, lifting his head and searching her eyes.

'Yes. I'm absolutely sure.'

'Then let's do it, and soon, before the baby comes.'

She nodded slowly, snuggling in against his side. 'Can we have a simple wedding? I don't really want a lot of fuss. It's not as if I've got any family, just a few friends.'

'Me, too. Well, other than my parents and my brother. A small, simple wedding sounds perfect,' he said, and she remembered his comment about Kerry and the endless trivia, and was glad she'd said what she had. She didn't want their wedding spoilt by comparisons, even if the other one had never happened.

'Even if it's going to be small, I suppose we'll need to choose a venue,' she said doubtfully, and he just smiled, a slow, sexy smile that made her heart race.

'Can we talk about that later? Right now, I really fancy an early night, and we've got the perfect venue for that right here.'

* * *

He led her up to the attic, to the huge mahogany bed, the bedding almost luminous in the moonlight. He didn't turn the lights on. He didn't need to. He could see everything he needed to without them.

He undressed her slowly, his hands tracing the changes brought about by her advancing pregnancy—the fullness of her breasts, the smooth, firm curve below them where their daughter lay safe and snug, awaiting her time.

He matched the curve with his hands, fingers outstretched, and felt a subtle shift beneath them, a tiny kick against his palm. It made him smile.

'Shut your eyes, little girl, you're not old enough for this,' he murmured, and stripped off his clothes, turning back to Kate to draw her into his arms. The warmth of her skin, silky soft, smooth under his hands, the firmness of her belly, the soft fullness of her breasts—they intoxicated him, making him feel drugged with happiness, swept away by the beauty and the honesty of her body.

He lowered his head and kissed her, and felt her catch fire, her hands searching his body, urgency replacing reverence as he laid her down in the huge and wonderful bed they'd chosen together.

And soon it would become their marriage bed.

He couldn't remember ever feeling this happy, this complete in all his life. It was his last coherent thought before the wildfire raging inside him engulfed them both.

'Can we get married here?'

They were sitting on the veranda, drinking coffee from the wonderful built-in machine James had had installed and had grieved about leaving behind, and nibbling pastries for breakfast.

It felt wonderfully decadent, almost honeymoon-like, but they had plans to make soon if she didn't want to be so far into her pregnancy that she waddled down the aisle.

'I don't think it's legal.'

'No, probably not. Can we do the ceremony paperwork somewhere else and then come back here for the party?'

'Then we can't leave, and I might want to get you on your own.'

'Oh, might you?' she said, laughing softly and batting his hands away as he explored her body yet again.

'Yes, I might. I might want to do it now.'

'Behave. You've got to go to work in a minute. Can we have a sensible conversation about this?'

'We've had that conversation. I think we should have the party elsewhere, so we can escape—and anyway, the weather might be wet, you can't be sure. Is there anywhere here with a smallish function room we could hire?'

'Zacharelli's?' she suggested. 'Although it's probably hideously expensive.'

'Let's find out,' he said, and glanced at his watch. 'Oh, damn, I have to go, I'm supposed to be there in ten minutes. You could try ringing them. See what dates they've got.'

He dropped his feet to the floor, kissed her goodbye and grabbed his car keys. 'I'll see you later.'

'OK. See you.'

She watched him drive away, feeling warm and fuzzy inside, and sat back, letting the fresh June morning air fill her lungs for a few more minutes before she cleared away their breakfast things and went and wrote, of all things calcu-lated to make Sam laugh his head off, a to-do list.

'So, I've got some dates for Zacharelli's,' she said when she caught up with Sam in the ED later. 'They haven't got any Saturdays except one in four weeks because they've had a cancel-lation. Is that too soon?'

'Probably not. We need to sort it with the reg-istrar. I'm due a break, I'll ring them. Can you give me the exact date?'

She handed him her notes, and he raised his eyebrows and stifled a smile. 'Is this a to-do list?' he asked carefully, and she closed her eyes and tried to look offended.

'You are so rude.'

His lips twitched. 'Surely not. OK, leave it with me. Did you get any prices?'

'They're emailing me.'

'OK. So once we've got it confirmed, we need to tell people. Do you want to draw up your guest list?'

'It'll take me all of two minutes.'

'How about your foster parents?' he suggested, his voice gentle.

She shrugged. 'I don't know. I owe them so much, but it's sort of difficult.'

'I know. Think about it, though, and maybe at least tell them.'

She nodded slowly, then glanced at the clock. 'I'd better get on. I'm due in Minors. I'll let you know what I find out.'

He dropped a kiss on her lips, winked at her and sauntered off, and James, coming round the corner at that moment, raised an eyebrow at her.

'Tut-tut, public displays of affection in the workplace,' he murmured, but she could see he was smiling.

'How's the house?' she asked.

'Chaotic. Congratulations, by the way. Sam tells me you're getting married.'

'Yes. I can't quite believe it, really. How's Connie?'

'Getting bigger. Only ten weeks to go now. Why don't you both come over and see the house and have a drink with us this evening?'

'Oh. OK. I'll have to check with Sam—'

'I'll do that, I'll see him in a minute. Are you

in Minors? There's a man in there I'm not happy about. Ryan Jarrold. He's got abdominal pain, but nothing showed on the ultrasound so we're waiting for a CT. Can you keep an eye on him and page me if you're concerned? I'll be back in a bit to check on him. And hustle CT.'

'Sure. Will do.'

It turned out that he was right to be worried, because five minutes after she arrived at Ryan's bedside, he broke out in a cold, clammy sweat and was rushed into Resus.

'He said he's been feeling rough for a couple of weeks,' she told James. 'Especially if he's hungry or after he's eaten a big meal.'

'Could be a bleeding ulcer. Right, let's get some fluids into him stat and see what we can find out.'

It was a perforated duodenal ulcer that, left neglected, had given him peritonitis and a massive intra-abdominal bleed, so the surgeon had told James later that afternoon, but they'd managed to save him.

'He was a lucky man,' James said. 'If that had happened at home, he might not have made it, and if Kate hadn't spotted the change in him so fast, we could still have lost him.'

'It was pretty obvious,' she said, but it still made her feel good to know she'd been appreciated.

They were standing in the garden of James and Connie's house, the sea at their backs and a renovation opportunity in front of them, and Kate was massively glad they hadn't taken on anything drastic like that.

'And I thought my boat was bad,' Sam said, eyeing it warily.

'It'll be fine. We can take it bit by bit,' Connie said placidly. 'At least it's clean now and we can live in it and work out what to do. Anyway, enough. Tell us about your wedding! It's much more interesting. When's it going to be?'

'Four weeks on Saturday,' Sam said. 'We're getting married at the Register Office at five, and then going down to Zacharelli's for the party. We've booked the function room, and I think we're going to have a buffet and an open bar.'

'Yowch. Do you trust your friends that much?' James said with a laugh, and Sam chuckled.

'It'll be fine. I'll make sure they're not too well stocked.'

'So, what are you going to wear?' Connie asked, looking at Kate. 'You'll need a wedding dress.'

Sam frowned slightly. 'I thought you didn't want a lot of fuss?'

'I don't—'

'Oh, come on, she's got to wear something, Sam! It doesn't have to be a meringue with foaming acres of tulle, but she'll still need a dress.'

Kate was hardly listening, because something about Sam's face was making her uneasy. Because of Kerry's wedding dress? She could hardly ask him, though, especially then and there, so she filed it for later.

'I doubt if it'll be a traditional one,' she said to reassure him. 'I'll be six months pregnant by then.'

'There are loads of pregnant brides these days,' Connie said, flapping her hand. 'They make some fabulous dresses.'

But Sam was still looking uneasy, and she changed the subject.

'Talking of babies, will you be upset if we paint the nursery?' she asked Connie.

'Of course not! He'd outgrown it anyway. Do you know what you're having?'

'A girl.'

'Oh, that's lovely! So are we!'

'Well, it balances Annie's two boys,' she said with a laugh, and the conversation moved on and Sam seemed to relax again, but she still had an uneasy feeling, and she tackled him about it when they got home.

'Talk to me about the wedding dress,' she said gently as he was getting into bed.

He froze for a second, then turned off the light and lay down on his back, staring at the ceiling. She rolled towards him.

'Sam?

'It's nothing.'

'No, it's not nothing. Tell me.'

'She never got to wear it,' he said, after a pause that seemed to stretch out into the hereafter. 'It was hanging in the wardrobe in the flat, and I gave it to the funeral directors. She was wearing it when we buried her.'

'Oh, Sam.' She wriggled closer, resting her

head on his shoulder and her hand over his heart. 'I'm sorry. I won't wear a dress.'

'No. You can wear whatever you want to, Kate. It doesn't matter. Just—maybe not lace.'

His eyes were closed, squeezed shut, and in the light of the moon she could see the thin, silver trail of a tear running down into his hair.

She wiped it away and kissed him, and he turned towards her and made love to her with a desperation that broke her heart.

The next four weeks flew by.

Annie and the babies came home from hospital, and she and Sam went over there for a barbeque so they could meet him properly. Ed of course had already met Sam at work, but they started talking boats and that was that, so she and Annie talked babies and discussed the wedding.

'I don't think I want my foster parents to come,' she confessed. 'It's a part of my life I want to forget.'

'Maybe your wedding's not the right time,' Annie said sagely. 'Why not leave it till afterwards, and contact them then.'

She nodded. 'Yes. Yes, that makes sense. You will be able to come, won't you?'

Annie laughed. 'Just try and keep me away. Do you want to stay here the night before? You can get ready here—and you can keep the dress here, when you get it.'

She didn't want to talk about the dress, not with Sam in earshot, so she just nodded and thanked her, and let it go.

CHAPTER ELEVEN

THE DAY OF the wedding dawned bright and clear and sunny.

A good omen? She wasn't sure. There was a tightness in her chest, an unnamed fear that wouldn't go away, and it stayed with her all day.

She'd stayed at Annie and Ed's because she was traditional enough to want to do it properly, and she'd spent the morning having a lovely facial that should have been relaxing, and her nails were painted in readiness, and then that afternoon the hairdresser had come to Annie's to put her hair up, but it didn't feel right.

Nothing felt right.

Not the hair, not the nails—certainly not the dress that she'd agonised over so much.

She'd gone shopping for it alone, because it was such a difficult issue what with Sam's feelings being so intricately involved in the subject, and it certainly wasn't lace, but it was still unmistakeably a wedding dress.

She stood at the bedroom window in Annie's house, staring out across the clifftop at the sea and thinking about Sam. Was he staring at it, too, down in their house by the harbour? What was he thinking about this, the wedding day that never should have been, or about the wedding that had never happened?

Annie tapped on her bedroom door. 'Can I come in?'

She opened the door, and Annie took one look at her face and hugged her.

'Oh, Kate, sweetheart, what's the matter? I thought you were happy?'

'I was, but now...I don't think I can do this. I don't think he's ready, Annie.'

'Nonsense. If he wasn't, he would never have asked you.'

'Yes, he would. He asked me on the day he found out I was pregnant, only the second time I'd ever met him. He's just being noble, doing the right thing, ticking the right box. He says he's old-fashioned and thinks a baby's parents should be married. I said no the first time he asked me, and the second, just a few weeks ago, and then when we found out it was a girl, and it all seemed real, I just said let's get married, but it was only a few days later, and maybe it really was too soon. Nothing had really changed, and when we talked about the dress—'

'What about it?' Annie prompted, so she told her what Sam had said about Kerry, and Annie sighed softly and hugged her.

'Darling girl, that doesn't mean he doesn't love you, just that he loved her, too, and it was desperately sad, what happened to him. It doesn't stop him loving you.'

'But he doesn't! He's had endless opportunities to tell me that he does, and he hasn't. Not once. And I can't bear to marry him when he doesn't love me,' she said, and the sob that was jammed in her throat broke free and she sank down onto the floor and cried her heart out.

Sam was standing in their bedroom gazing blindly out to sea and wondering how he'd got to be so lucky when his phone rang.

He stared at it, a feeling of foreboding creeping into him and chilling him to the bone. 'Hello?'

'Sam, it's Annie. You need to come.'

Fear coursed through him. 'Why? What's happened? Is she all right?'

'She's fine,' Annie said quickly, and he hauled in a breath. 'She's fine, but—Sam, she needs to see you, to talk to you. She's having a wobble about the wedding.'

'What? OK, OK, I'll come. Just—don't let her go anywhere.'

He ran downstairs, grabbed his car keys, locked the door as an afterthought and drove the two minutes up the road to Annie and Ed's in a minute flat, abandoning the car on the drive.

Ed opened the door and let him in. 'They're upstairs in the front bedroom on the right. Take a deep breath.'

He paused, catching his breath, trying to slow his heart but it was still racing, the dread clinging to him like a mantle.

'Why?' he breathed, and Ed laid a hand on his shoulder.

'I think she just needs your reassurance.'

He nodded, hauled in another breath and forced himself to walk slowly up the stairs. Annie was on the landing, standing by the open bedroom door, and she patted his shoulder and left him to it.

Kate was sitting on the floor in a puddle of pale grey silk, and the sight of her nearly broke his heart.

He reached out his hands and pulled her gently to her feet. Her eyes were puffy from crying, and she had a wad of crumpled, soggy tissues in one hand. He took them from her, steered her to the bed and sat down beside her, her hands held firmly in his.

'Kate, whatever's the matter, sweetheart? Talk to me—tell me what's wrong.'

Where did she start?

'I can't do it,' she said, blinking away tears and trying her hardest not to cry. 'I can't marry you, Sam. You're just doing it to be noble, because you're that sort of man, kind and decent and honourable, and you think this is all your fault, but I can't let you do it, because it won't work, and when it all goes wrong and you leave me—'

'I won't. I've told you that and I don't renege on my promises.'

'But you can't know that. What if it gets unbearable? Or is it that you're so dead inside that you don't really care what happens because you can't feel it anyway?'

Emotions flickered over his face so fast she couldn't read them, but she recognised enough to know it might be true.

She eased her hands away from him and stood up, walking over to the window and clinging to the frame for support. 'Sam, I can't. I can't marry you when I know you don't love me, can't marry you just to ease your guilty conscience. I don't want to be your consolation prize, someone there for you to distract you from your grief while you go through the motions, while all the time you're secretly wishing I was Kerry.'

She turned and met his shocked eyes.

'I'm sorry I'm not her, I'm sorry it's not her here in her lovely lace dress, having your baby, planning a future with you in your lovely new house, but I'm not her, I'm me, and I can't marry you just so that you can play happy families and pretend to yourself that it's all OK. Even I know I'm worth more than that.'

'But—Kate…'

'Kate nothing, Sam,' she said heavily. 'I'm not

going to enter into a loveless marriage. I've seen enough of them in my life, and I don't intend to be part of one. I'm sorry—'

'It's not loveless. Not on my part, at least.'

He got up and walked over to her, taking her hands again, staring down at her with eyes so sincere she almost believed him. 'I didn't expect this. When you told me you were pregnant, all I could think about was doing the right thing. You were right about that. But in the last few weeks, somehow—I don't understand how, because I never thought it would ever happen to me again, but I've grown to love you. I think I started to love you when you decided to keep the baby, because it was such a hard decision for you, a really difficult and courageous choice to make, and I had to ask you to trust me when you really didn't know me, and yet you did it. You put your future in my hands, and in doing so you gave me a future, too, something to look forward to where there'd been nothing.

'Do you know, I woke up this morning feeling happy, with everything I'd ever wanted? Marrying a beautiful woman who I love, who's carrying my child, a job in a fabulous place, a stunning house overlooking the sea we both love—the only fly in the ointment is that you don't love me. I always knew you were going for the safe option out of fear and a need for security, and I can't blame you, not with your childhood, but I can work with that and hope that, given time, you'll come to love me, too, as much as I love you.'

She stared at him, wanting so much to believe it, unable to dare. 'No. You love Kerry, Sam,' she said sadly. 'You can't let her go.'

'I can. I have. Yes, Kerry will always be a part of my past, and she'll always hold a part of my heart, because I did love her, and I can't just turn that off, but it doesn't hurt any more in the way it did. I'm still sad for her that her life was cut so cruelly short, but you're my life now.

'I love you, Katherine Ashton, and I love our baby, too. I'll love you both to the end of my days, whether you marry me or not. That won't change. But I won't force you to do something you're unhappy about, and if you really feel that you don't love me, and my love isn't enough to make this work for you—'

'Why haven't you told me? If you love me, why haven't you told me?'

He gave a sad little laugh. 'I only really realised it today. I was going to tell you right before we got married. It was stupid of me. I should have told you before, I should have rung you. I'm sorry. But you haven't told me, either, and maybe that's why I was holding back.'

'Oh, Sam—of course I love you, but I was afraid to say so. I didn't want to give too much of myself away because I thought you weren't ready to hear it, and I was trying to save myself from any more hurt—'

His arms closed round her, crushing her against his chest.

'Silly girl,' he said raggedly, and his chest heaved with emotion as he held her there and told her, again and again, that he loved her.

And finally she believed him.

She eased away, trying to smile at him through her tears. 'Well, if we're going to do this we'd better hurry,' she said, and he pulled her back into his arms for one last, quick hug before he let her go.

'You need to sort out your makeup,' he said

with a wry grin, and she ran over to the mirror and wailed, dabbing at her tear-stained face.

'I look a wreck!'

'You look beautiful. Just a little streaky.'

He smiled at her in the mirror, and she smiled back, dabbing at her cheeks.

'Give me two seconds.'

It took a little more than that, mostly because her hands were shaking, but then she turned to him and smiled unsteadily.

'There. How do I look? Will I do?'

He pressed his lips together hard, and swallowed.

'You look lovely,' he said gruffly. 'Absolutely beautiful. I'm so proud of you.'

His voice cracked, and she put her arms around him and hugged him. 'Oh, Sam. Are you OK?'

He nodded, looked down at her and smiled tenderly.

'Never better. I love you,' he said again, just in case she hadn't quite got it yet, and then, taking her by the hand, he led her out of the house.

The wedding was wonderful.

Quiet, of course, with so few guests, but they

were the people who mattered. James and Connie, Ed and Annie, Sam's parents and his brother, a few old friends—and her foster parents, who she'd finally contacted just a few days before, because of all the people in her past, they were the only ones she loved and who loved her.

They'd hugged her and cried, and Sam had to find a box of tissues to mop them all up, and then they moved to Zaccharelli's for the party. She was standing outside on the balcony overlooking the sea when Sam came up behind her and slid his arms around her, resting his hands on the baby.

'OK?'

'Definitely. You?'

'Mmm. Only one thing could make it better.' He turned her into his arms. 'The car's here. Ready to go home?'

'Absolutely.'

They ran the gauntlet of the confetti, scrambled into the car and snuggled up in the back for the short journey to the house.

He helped her out, tipped the driver and led her up the veranda steps, then he unlocked the door, swept her up into his arms and kissed her.

'Sam!' she squealed, wrapping her arms firmly round his neck for safety. 'What are you doing?'

'What I should have done weeks ago,' he said, and he carried her over the threshold, setting her carefully back on her feet in the hall.

'Welcome home, Mrs Ryder,' he said gruffly, and she went up on tiptoe and kissed him.

'Thank you,' she whispered. 'Thank you for everything. I never thought I could ever be this happy. I love you, Sam. I love you so much.'

'I love you, too.' He kissed her back, slowly and thoroughly, then lifted his head and gazed down into her eyes. 'Do you think you can manage to walk upstairs to bed?' he murmured with a mischievous smile, and she laughed and took his hand and went with him up to the attic.

He turned on the lamps, revealing their beautiful bed strewn with rose petals, and emotion choked her.

'You old romantic,' she said unevenly, touched almost to tears, and he drew her into his arms and kissed her again.

'I thought you'd like it. I wanted to make you happy, today of all days.'

'You did. You do. Every day of my life. Now stop stalling and make love to me, Mr Ryder.'
He chuckled softly. 'It'll be a pleasure.'

EPILOGUE

'I CAN'T BELIEVE you've sold her.'

Sam stood at the top of the veranda steps, and watched as the boat, carefully loaded onto a trailer, was towed slowly away, and he realised that all he felt was pride in the restoration work he'd done over the summer, and relief that it was over.

'She's served her purpose,' he said softly, moving to sit beside her in the glorious October sunshine. 'If it hadn't been for her, I wouldn't have met you that night, and we wouldn't be sitting here now.'

'Are you sure?'

He took his eyes off the boat and turned to face her. 'Yeah. Why would we?'

'Because James and Connie asked you to come, as a favour?'

He smiled thoughtfully. 'I've wondered about

that. I think I probably would have come, so I would have met you.'

'But James warned us both off, so maybe it wouldn't have gone any further.'

Sam chuckled. 'Seriously? I struggled to keep my hands off you while we were trying to make some fundamental and life-changing decisions, so I'm pretty sure we would have had an affair, at least.'

'But I wouldn't have got pregnant. It was the perfect storm—if you hadn't broken your golden rule, and I hadn't had the bug, it wouldn't have happened, and there would have been nothing tying us together, nothing to hold you here in Yoxburgh.'

'Nothing except love,' he said softly, wrapping his arm around her and resting his head against hers. 'And that might have happened anyway, but we did have the perfect storm, and we have a beautiful, perfect little baby who we really need to find a name for.'

Kate's eyes went back to the boat. 'How about Isadora?'

'Isadora?' His eyes traced the name he'd lovingly repainted on her stern. 'Why?'

She smiled fondly, her eyes misting. 'We owe her everything,' she said, 'and anyway, it's a beautiful name.'

'Isadora,' he said, tasting it, and then he nodded. 'Yes. Yes, it is. I like it. How about a middle name?'

Kate hesitated. 'I thought—maybe Rose? For my mother? I don't know why she left me or what happened to her, and I probably never will, but I know that she loved me, I remember that, and now that I'm a mother, I know it must have been the hardest thing in the world to do, to let me go into school that day knowing she'd never see me again.'

'Maybe you would have been in danger? Maybe she was in some kind of trouble.'

'I think she must have been, and it's only now, when I realise just what love is, that I can forgive her because I know what a sacrifice she made for me.'

Sam hugged her closer and pressed a kiss to her hair. 'I think it would be lovely to call the baby Rose.'

'Not for her first name, but just there, so I remember her.'

He felt his eyes fill, and blinked.

'Isadora Rose. It's beautiful.'

He looked down at her, lying asleep in her mother's arms, her mouth a perfect rosebud, and he leant over and feathered his lips against her downy head, then settled back, his arm around his wife, and watched as the boat disappeared from their lives, her job done.

* * * * *

If you enjoyed this story,
check out these other great reads
from Caroline Anderson

RISK OF A LIFETIME
THE SECRET IN HIS HEART
BEST FRIEND TO WIFE AND MOTHER
SNOWED IN WITH THE BILLIONAIRE

All available now!

MILLS & BOON®
Large Print Medical

September

Their Secret Royal Baby	Carol Marinelli
Her Hot Highland Doc	Annie O'Neil
His Pregnant Royal Bride	Amy Ruttan
Baby Surprise for the Doctor Prince	Robin Gianna
Resisting Her Army Doc Rival	Sue MacKay
A Month to Marry the Midwife	Fiona McArthur

October

Their One Night Baby	Carol Marinelli
Forbidden to the Playboy Surgeon	Fiona Lowe
A Mother to Make a Family	Emily Forbes
The Nurse's Baby Secret	Janice Lynn
The Boss Who Stole Her Heart	Jennifer Taylor
Reunited by Their Pregnancy Surprise	Louisa Heaton

November

Mummy, Nurse...Duchess?	Kate Hardy
Falling for the Foster Mum	Karin Baine
The Doctor and the Princess	Scarlet Wilson
Miracle for the Neurosurgeon	Lynne Marshall
English Rose for the Sicilian Doc	Annie Claydon
Engaged to the Doctor Sheikh	Meredith Webber

MILLS & BOON®
Large Print Medical

December

Healing the Sheikh's Heart	Annie O'Neil
A Life-Saving Reunion	Alison Roberts
The Surgeon's Cinderella	Susan Carlisle
Saved by Doctor Dreamy	Dianne Drake
Pregnant with the Boss's Baby	Sue MacKay
Reunited with His Runaway Doc	Lucy Clark

January

The Surrogate's Unexpected Miracle	Alison Roberts
Convenient Marriage, Surprise Twins	Amy Ruttan
The Doctor's Secret Son	Janice Lynn
Reforming the Playboy	Karin Baine
Their Double Baby Gift	Louisa Heaton
Saving Baby Amy	Annie Claydon

February

Tempted by the Bridesmaid	Annie O'Neil
Claiming His Pregnant Princess	Annie O'Neil
A Miracle for the Baby Doctor	Meredith Webber
Stolen Kisses with Her Boss	Susan Carlisle
Encounter with a Commanding Officer	Charlotte Hawkes
Rebel Doc on Her Doorstep	Lucy Ryder

MILLS & BOON®
Large Print – September 2017

ROMANCE

The Sheikh's Bought Wife	Sharon Kendrick
The Innocent's Shameful Secret	Sara Craven
The Magnate's Tempestuous Marriage	Miranda Lee
The Forced Bride of Alazar	Kate Hewitt
Bound by the Sultan's Baby	Carol Marinelli
Blackmailed Down the Aisle	Louise Fuller
Di Marcello's Secret Son	Rachael Thomas
Conveniently Wed to the Greek	Kandy Shepherd
His Shy Cinderella	Kate Hardy
Falling for the Rebel Princess	Ellie Darkins
Claimed by the Wealthy Magnate	Nina Milne

HISTORICAL

The Secret Marriage Pact	Georgie Lee
A Warriner to Protect Her	Virginia Heath
Claiming His Defiant Miss	Bronwyn Scott
Rumours at Court (Rumors at Court)	Blythe Gifford
The Duke's Unexpected Bride	Lara Temple

MEDICAL

Their Secret Royal Baby	Carol Marinelli
Her Hot Highland Doc	Annie O'Neil
His Pregnant Royal Bride	Amy Ruttan
Baby Surprise for the Doctor Prince	Robin Gianna
Resisting Her Army Doc Rival	Sue MacKay
A Month to Marry the Midwife	Fiona McArthur

0817 GEN STD LP